The Royal Diaries

×◆×

Isabel

×◆×◆×

Jewel of Castilla

BY CAROLYN MEYER

Scholastic Inc. New York

Segovia — 19th of February 1466
Ash Wednesday

Since midnight I have knelt for hours on the stone floor and taken only water and a little bread. The sun has not yet climbed above the castle walls, but my back aches, and my stomach feels as hollow as a drum. The royal chapel is so cold that my lips are numb. I fear my prayers are too chilled to fly to God's ear.

Lent has begun, forty days of prayer and fasting. This morning before dawn, my confessor, Tomás de Torquemada, assigned me an extra penance. The priest summoned me after Mass and gave me this small book. The white parchment pages are blank. I am to examine my conscience regularly. Whenever I commit a Deadly Sin, I am to write it here and meditate upon it.

"To record the sin is to be aware of it, and to be aware of the sin is to avoid it," he said, glowering down at me.

"How long must I do this, Padre?" I asked him.

"Until your soul is no longer in danger of the flames of Hell," he said in a voice that seemed to come from the grave.

Padre Torquemada likes to scare people. Thin as a knife blade, face gaunt as a skeleton's, eyes burning like hot coals, he does frighten me.

I shall call it my Book of Deadly Sins.

Here is my first one: ANGER.

The cause of my anger is my brother's wife, Queen Juana. She is a vain and silly creature who would rather dance and flirt with her courtiers and play at cards with her ladies-in-waiting than pay attention to her own child. It has been a year since my elder brother, Enrique, King of Castilla, banished me here to Segovia, to live in this castle with the Queen and her little daughter, also called Juana, titled Princess of Asturias. Meanwhile Enrique stays at court in Madrid, so he does not witness his wife's improper behavior.

It is surely plain to anyone that Queen Juana's conduct is scandalous. It was plain enough to our younger brother, Alfonso. He was so outraged by the revealing gowns worn by the Queen's ladies-in-waiting that he once ordered them not to associate with me. Of course everyone laughed at him, then only a boy of nine. That was four years ago, and she and her ladies have become no more modest in their attire.

Did Padre Torquemada also give the Queen a book in which to record her sins? If he did, her book will be filled long before mine.

Segovia — 25th of February 1466

PRIDE is said to be the worst of the Seven Deadly Sins. I am guilty. Here is the explanation.

Enrique has come to visit us. Queen Juana appeared in a silk gown cut low to show off her bosom, powdered white and perched like a pair of plump doves. She paints her cheeks with circles of rouge and dangles jewels from her ears, even in this solemn season. The King arrived dressed, as usual, in his rough jerkin and coarse leggings and muddy boots. And in need of bathing, or at least some perfumery! My maid, Ana, helped me dress in a woolen gown and caught up my hair in a plain net. I wore no jewels.

King Enrique is my half brother. He was already a

grown man when his mother died and our father, Juan, King of Castilla, wed my mother, the Princess Isabel of Portugal. I was born three years later, my brother Alfonso not two years after that. When our father died, Enrique became king. Alfonso was still a babe in our mother's arms. My mother, now called the Queen Widow, took us to spend our days quietly in a plain little castle in the country town of Arévalo.

But King Enrique did not allow us children to stay with our mother. First he ordered us to live at court in Madrid, which we despised for its sinful ways. Later he sent us here, to Segovia, a day's journey from Madrid through the mountains. For weeks after our arrival, Enrique kept Alfonso locked up in a castle tower, and freed him only after he learned that Queen Juana had tried to poison Alfonso with herbs. She wanted to get rid of Alfonso, because she is determined that her daughter, Princess Juana, will one day inherit the throne from King Enrique — even though it is not the custom for queens to rule in our kingdom!

I am sure that Enrique regrets letting Alfonso go. Two years ago many of the *grandes*, the most powerful nobles of the kingdom, became disgusted with Enrique. They say that he is weak and indecisive. But they are like little kings themselves, always fighting over petty jealousies. Every powerful man has an army. Even the bishops have armies. To stop the feuding, some of these *grandes* and churchmen set up a rebel throne and placed my younger brother upon it, proclaiming him King Alfonso. Now Castilla has two kings, the kingdom is divided, and the people do not know which king to serve.

King Enrique orders me to remain here. "For your safety," he says, although it is he who has many enemies. Though the castle is richly adorned with silver and gold, it still feels like a prison. And he has summoned me to sup with him tonight. I do not look forward to it with pleasure.

Segovia — 26th of February 1466

This is what happened last night. After a Lenten meal of baked fish, Queen Juana took her leave. (I suspect she had friends to entertain at cards.) I stayed at table with my brother.

"So, little sister," Enrique began, rubbing his reddened eyelids, "soon you will observe your fifteenth birthday." Sprawling in his chair, the King belched loudly.

"On the twenty-second of April," I said, and lowered my eyes modestly, as a lady must.

"I am making you a gift of Trujillo," he continued. What he meant is that I will receive rents and taxes from the town of Trujillo, the sum of ninety gold pieces a year.

I thanked him very much and kissed his hand (trying to ignore his dirty fingernails) and assured him that he was the best and most generous brother. (This is not true, but untruth is not one of the Deadly Sins, and so I need not record it here.)

"Old enough to wed," Enrique continued. He pulled out a gold toothpick and began to clean his teeth — too late, I think, for his breath was foul.

"Yes, My Lord," I replied, sweet as honey, although I dreaded what was coming.

"High time, then, to find you a husband. It will please you that King Afonso of Portugal finds you very attractive. He would have you as his wife, if you give your consent."

This was exactly what I feared. Often before, Enrique

has spoken of betrothing me to King Afonso, the repulsive brother of Queen Juana. Afonso is rich and powerful, and that is why Enrique wants me to marry him. That the Portuguese king is more than twice my age and ugly as a scorpion matters not a bit to my brother!

And what if I do not consent? I wanted to shout at him. But I knelt before my brother the King and, keeping my head bowed so that he would not see my tears, answered, "As My Lord wishes."

Now to explain why I am guilty of the sin of PRIDE: I am only a lesser princess, not in line to inherit the throne (it will go to Enrique's son, if he ever has one; otherwise, to our brother Alfonso — NOT to Princess Juana). Yet I believe that I am too good to marry the King of Portugal. *El Escorpión*, I call him — the Scorpion.

Segovia — 27th of February 1466

After Mass today I shut myself in my chambers and hoped that Enrique would not send for me again. I passed the hours reading in my Bible and did not come out until I saw him ride off with his courtiers. How poor he looked in his rude clothes, with not even a ruffed linen collar to

7

show that he is anything but a humble peasant. (Surely this is an example of SLOTH, seventh and last of the Deadly Sins!) I do wonder that Queen Juana puts up with him, unwashed and bad smelling as he is. And he with her, with her paints and perfumes! It unnerves me that the man he wants me to marry is the Queen's brother.

Since Enrique left I have spent hours on my knees, begging God's forgiveness for my sins and asking His help. *O Lord, deliver me from marriage to El Escorpión!*

Segovia — 1st of March 1466

Dear Clara, my nurse-governess, does what she can to lift my spirits. She herself is Portuguese, as is my poor mother, whose spirits seem not to be lifted by anyone. Since my father's death a dozen years ago, my mother has closeted herself in a dark and silent place. Even when I am with her, she is beyond my reach, gazing at me with empty, haunted eyes.

"Your mother has often told me she hoped you would one day marry a Portuguese," Clara coaxed. "All that gold from Africa has made King Afonso very wealthy. It would be a wise marriage for you, Doña Isabel. And you already speak the language well."

"But Clara," I wailed, "have you never seen the man? He is old and ugly! Two years ago Enrique and the Queen took me to visit him. My brother wanted to betroth me to him then and there. But our father's will states plainly that Enrique may not marry me to anyone unless the *grandes* consent. Now I fear he will ignore our father's wishes and do as he pleases."

To which Clara could say nothing, except to remark that when I am angry, my looks are spoiled. If Enrique forces me to marry El Escorpión, my anger will turn my looks to sour milk indeed!

Segovia — 4th of March 1466

My ladies-in-waiting and I spent the day with our needle-work. I am stitching a shirt for my younger brother. I would enjoy this more if the ladies did not chatter so much — especially Blanca, who has a voice like a magpie. María speaks tiresomely of little else but the new gowns she is to have, Jimena stuffs her mouth constantly with sweets, Mencia is none too bright, and Elvira believes she is more intelligent than everyone. All of my ladies are the daughters or sisters of *grandes* who are Enrique's courtiers.

The only one whose company I truly enjoy is my friend Catalina Valera, whose father is Keeper of the Royal Treasury. Catalina draws beautifully with pen and ink. She is also skilled with a needle and has designed a banner, the Lamb of God on white silk. Above its head sits a golden crown stitched in gold thread. Her stitches are perfect.

Catalina is the most comely of the ladies. She has fine features and large brown eyes with brows as thick and black as sable. She is talented and beautiful, but she is also unlucky: Catalina has one leg shorter than the other with a misshapen foot, causing her to walk with a limp. I wonder if this is God's punishment upon her. She is of *converso* descent, Jews who converted to Christianity generations ago. There are rumors that the Valeras remain Jews at heart and practice the old ways in secret.

We are seldom alone, but today, when the others had flocked off somewhere for a short time, I confided to Catalina my fears of a betrothal to El Escorpión.

Catalina shook her head sympathetically. "I have no

words for you, Doña Isabel," she said. "I have already made up my mind to enter a convent and to devote my life to God."

"But why?"

"Because of my leg," she said, dark eyes brimming with tears. "My father has been unable to find a suitor for me, even with promises of a large marriage gift. And I have several sisters for whom husbands must be found."

I clasped her hands in mine and told her I was sorry. But secretly I sometimes wish I could trade places with her. Life with God sounds much better than life with El Escorpión.

And there, despite my good intentions, is another Deadly Sin: ENVY.

Segovia — 7th of March 1466

Little Princess Juana runs about, ignored by her mother and pursued by her nurse. Sometimes I keep her with me. I am her godmother, present at her birth four years ago, so this is my duty. It is not an unpleasant one. I am trying to teach her her stitches — backstitch, chain stitch, and so on — but she quickly loses patience, and so do I.

The Princess loves to visit the alabaster hall with the statues of the kings of Castilla. Thirty-four of them, carved of wood and painted in silver and gold, are seated on thrones, holding their scepters. Their queens stand behind them and a little to one side, a fact that has not gone unnoticed by the little Princess.

"Why are there no queens on the thrones?" she asked, and I explained that by tradition, queens do not rule. It is believed that women do not have the capacity to govern.

The last in the row of carvings is Enrique, looking much better in painted wood than he does in the flesh. The sculptor made him thinner, but his broken nose and jutting chin give him the same fierce countenance that he has in real life. I have heard him called *El León*, the Lion, and the name suits him.

Besides the kings, there is El Cid, the legendary knight who fought bravely and well for my ancestor King Alfonso VI four centuries ago. El Cid is my favorite statue. While the Princess climbs on the lap of Enrique's likeness, I gaze upon the conquering hero.

Enrique fears that if I am left to myself, some of his enemies — and he has many — may turn me against him.
And so I am watched at every step, forbidden to venture
beyond the walls of Segovia. I feel sure that some of my
ladies carry tales to their fathers and brothers, who then
report to Enrique. I suspect Elvira most of all, because of
her elevated opinion of herself, but it could just as well be
the dull Mencia. Only Catalina do I trust completely.

And what of my maid, Ana? The clumsy girl always
seems to barge in just as I begin to write in this book. It is
my good luck that she cannot read. What would she think
of this if she <u>could</u>?

Stout and ruddy-faced, Ana carries with her the fresh
air of the countryside. The sight of her makes me yearn for
the best times of my childhood, for she is little more than
a child herself. I was free then to ride my horse whenever
I wished, to hunt in the forest with Alfonso, and to wade
in the cool streams. All that ended when Enrique insisted
upon taking us to Madrid — to be educated, he said. And
who was placed in charge of my "education?" Queen
Juana! She makes a fine tutor in wantonness and bawdry.

Though I am here against my will, at least I am permitted certain visitors. My dear friend Beatríz de Bobadilla came yesterday from Arévalo. Her visits are rare, and therefore all the more precious.

Beatríz is twenty-three and betrothed to Andrés de Cabrera, Enrique's chief steward. We look enough alike to be taken for sisters. She is as tall as I am, slim-waisted, and fair-skinned. Her hair, like mine, is reddish gold, and her eyes, like mine, are between green and blue. What I most admire about Beatríz are her intelligence and her courage. She defies custom and always rides a horse rather than a mule, as is expected of young ladies once they are past childhood.

Soon after her arrival, Beatríz whispered, "I must speak with you in private." But to avoid drawing the attention of my ladies, we forced ourselves to sit among them with our needlework in our laps, our tongues moving faster than our needles, chattering about her coming wedding.

Eventually, Beatríz and I wrapped ourselves in our cloaks and strolled about the castle yard. We were under the watchful eyes of the sentries in the turrets that loom high above the thick walls, but I was certain that our words could not be overheard.

"I am worried about King Alfonso," she whispered. "Word comes from Ávila that he is losing support."

"Is there nothing to be done?" I asked, but I know the answer. I am helpless to help him.

Although he is only thirteen, my younger brother, King Alfonso, takes his role seriously, as he should. And my older brother, King Enrique, is determined to keep the crown and the throne for himself. I try to appear not to favor either one. My sympathies are with my younger brother, but for my own safety I must not anger the elder. It is a terrible position to be in, pulled this way and that.

Everyone believes Enrique has decided that upon his death, the true crown of Castilla should pass to Alfonso. That would seem the proper thing to do, for Enrique as yet has no son. But "the proper thing" means nothing to Queen Juana. She has made up her mind that her little Princess will one day rule as the first Queen of Castilla, no matter what tradition dictates.

This is surely the sin of AVARICE!

Why is it that STUPIDITY is not one of the Deadly Sins?

Segovia — 14th of March 1466

Beatríz mounted her horse and rode off with her escort only hours ago. Before taking her leave, she asked, "What about El Escorpión? Has Enrique yet betrothed you to him?" I had not wanted to talk about it until then.

"Not yet, but I know that soon I may be forced to yield." Suddenly I burst into tears. "How I do envy you," I wept, "to be betrothed to a man you do not despise!"

(ENVY! Again!)

Since she has gone I am downcast and shaken.

Segovia — 15th of March 1466

If writing in this book is meant to cure me of my sins, it is a failure. I know that it is not for me to accuse another of sin, as I did when I wrote the other day of Queen Juana. Even if it be true. I shall confess to Padre Torquemada and accept the penance he assigns me.

It is well known that the padre's own life is one of constant penance. He wears a hair shirt next to his skin, sleeps on a wooden board, eats no meat, denies himself all food for days at a time — this for his soul's good. I hate to have him order my penance, even if it be for <u>my</u> soul's good.

Segovia — 18th of March 1466

My penance is to fast until Easter, eating only enough to sustain life, but not enough to satisfy appetite. Our Lenten meals are spare enough — plain fish or eggs but once a day, and bread and fruit for supper. But I am to deny myself even those and may eat only vegetables for two weeks. Especially eggplant, which I loathe. And cabbage, worse. No artichokes, just because I love them. No oranges for the same reason. I may not succeed in conquering my sin of PRIDE, but I shall certainly feel the pangs of hunger when I retire to my bed after a supper of nothing but bread and onions.

Three weeks of such fare.

Ana, the dear child, has told me that she has made up her mind to share my "suffering," as she puts it. So, bread and onions for her, too.

Segovia — 21st of March 1466

Poor Ana. The onions cause her distress, and she goes about with a pinched look. I brought her a bit of fish from the table, which she at first refused and then devoured hungrily.

Segovia — 23rd of March 1466

Queen Juana came last evening to speak to me very seriously about my betrothal to her brother, the King of Portugal. As I was finishing my prayers, she appeared in my chambers with no regard for my modesty. As usual the Queen was dressed in a tight-waisted gown that squeezed up her breasts, whereas I had to conduct the entire conversation wearing only my shift.

"Doña Isabel," she began, "I trust you will not oppose King Enrique's wish that you marry my brother."

I decided that silence was best and so made no reply. She strolled about my chamber, picking up various objects and setting them down again, pausing to admire a gold crucifix given to me by my mother. It was all I could do to keep from snatching it out of her hands.

"We are arranging your wedding in July, or perhaps August," she said. "Will you like that, Doña Isabel? A pretty summer wedding?"

"I will not like it at all!" I exclaimed. "Nor an autumn wedding, nor a winter wedding, nor a spring wedding. I have not liked the idea of a wedding to the King of Portugal from the first time I met him."

She seemed surprised. "But why?" she asked.

"He is much older than I, and I think that we have little in common." I did not mention El Escorpión's ugliness!

She frowned, her little red mouth pinched up in a pout. "King Enrique is many years older than I," she reminded me. "And your own father was much older than your mother. I believe it best that way." And then she grinned boldly and winked at me. "Just wait and see! With an old husband who falls asleep as soon as he has eaten his supper, you are free to amuse yourself. There are many handsome young men at court, all eager to please you, to fetch you a glass of wine, to place a cushion under your feet, to wear your ring when they ride their horses in a tournament joust. So you see, my dear little Isabel, it will all work out very well for you to wed my brother. You will have yourself a merry life at court in Lisbon."

Then, I am grateful to record, the scandalous woman left me alone with my thoughts. If ever there was a person guilty of LUST, surely it is Queen Juana.

Segovia — 26th of March 1466

Clara is a faithful governess but a shameless gossip. Yesterday I overheard her speaking with some of the ladies of the household about *"La Beltraneja."* They were talking about little Princess Juana. I pretended not to listen.

Rumors fly that King Enrique is not really the father of Princess Juana. It is whispered that her true father is Enrique's closest friend and adviser, Beltrán de la Cueva. Thus some have begun to call her "La Beltraneja" — the daughter of Beltrán.

I have studied Princess Juana closely while she sits by my side, deeply concentrating on the scrap of linen on which she is working a little bird in cross-stitch. I must say that she most closely resembles her mother — especially the saucy manner in which she rolls her eyes and flirtatiously cocks her head to one side. But it does seem she also carries some of the features of the handsome Cueva. It sickens me to think on this.

But then I think on <u>this</u>: If the child is not Enrique's true daughter, then she is not born of a legal marriage. If she is not born of a legal marriage, she cannot inherit the throne. It is that simple. No matter how much her mother plots and schemes, Princess Juana will never rule Castilla. The crown must go to my brother Alfonso, true son of the King of Castilla.

Still, Clara had best watch her tongue.

Segovia — 4th of April 1466
Good Friday

I, who am not without sin, shall not cast the first stone.
I, who am not without sin, shall not cast the first stone.
I, who am not without sin, shall not cast the first stone.

I could fill a whole book with this sentiment.

Before dawn Catalina and my other attendants accompanied me to the convent for Mass. Moved by the chanting of the nuns in their chapel, I recognized that I am guilty of even more sins, grave if not deadly. I have listened to ugly rumors about the Queen and her innocent child. And I have blamed others without examining my own conscience.

Therefore I shall not wait for Padre Torquemada to

hear my confession and prescribe a further penance. I have devised my own punishment: On the Great Feast of Easter, I shall feast only on lentils.

Segovia — 5th of April 1466

Preparations are under way for tomorrow's feast, under the shrill direction of Queen Juana.

Servants have scattered clean rushes on the stone floor of the Great Hall and have sprinkled them with sweet-smelling herbs and spices. Long wooden trestles are spread with cloths of spotless white linen and set with the castle's finest silver plates and goblets. Fires are laid and spits loaded with venison and wild boar. Beginning at dawn, the cooks' helpers will turn the spits as the meat roasts over the hot coals.

King Enrique is expected to ride out from Madrid with his courtiers. There will be many other guests as well, including my protector, Archbishop Carrillo.

A towering figure with heavy features and a deep, booming voice, the Archbishop reminds me of a great bull — secretly we call him *El Toro*. Although he looks fearsome,

I have a deep fondness for him. Carrillo was a kind counselor to Alfonso and me when we were children at Enrique's court in Madrid. He taught us to play chess. (I was a better player than Alfonso, who always cried when I won.)

I wish that Alfonso were going to be present, but of course he will not. Even if he were invited, he would fear Queen Juana's poison in his cup.

Segovia — 6th of April 1466
Easter Day

Alleluia, Christ is risen! He is risen indeed!

As I expected, the banquet was magnificent.

First Queen Juana swept in, gowned in scarlet satin with a lining of marten fur, her train dragging behind her and the collar of her cloak draped halfway down her back. Her hair was caught up in a net edged with white satin lilies embroidered in silver. She jangled an armful of jeweled bracelets and wore gold pendants in her ears. To show her piety, she carried a rosary of pearls and golden beads!

The little Princess was dressed almost as richly, in red velvet trimmed with lace and leaves of silver. And my brother King Enrique? He had not taken time to bathe or shave or even comb his bushy hair before coming straight to the table, still in his dusty black cloak. It appeared that he had just come in from prowling El Bazaín, his wild animal park. He keeps a collection of bears and ocelots and leopards and other creatures, including a mountain goat that he loves like a pet. King Enrique does look ever so much like a lion himself, but a shaggy old one, not the King of Beasts. Have I mentioned his hat, black and broad-brimmed, that he never removes? Perhaps he sleeps in it.

Archbishop Carrillo, resplendent in purple velvet and jewels, was accompanied by his scheming nephew, Juan Pacheco, a small, thin man with a quivering voice and a sly manner. My name for him is *El Zorro*, the Fox. I distrust him.

The feasting began, a parade of carvers slicing up the juicy meat from the spits and servers carrying it to the guests. The climax was the presentation of a roasted peacock on a golden platter, its tail feathers replaced and spread like a fan. A collar of gold cloth, painted with the King's coat of arms, was placed around its neck.

And there in the midst of all this plenty, I sat in a plain yellow gown, with my bowl of lentils.

My penitential meal was noted by Archbishop Carrillo. "Lentils, Doña Isabel?" he boomed, observing my poor portion. "On the Great Feast of Easter?"

Would it count as less of a penance if I spoke of it, I wondered? But, I reasoned, the Archbishop is a priest and a man of God (although I doubt that he wears a hair shirt or sleeps on a board), so I explained the purpose.

"I am a sinner, Your Grace," I said. "This is my penance."

"But we are all sinners," the Archbishop replied heartily. "And on this day of the Resurrection of Our Lord, even sinners must celebrate."

I pushed aside the bowl of lentils that I had been stirring without appetite and accepted a plate of venison and saffron rice and a dessert of pomegranate and almond cake, which I did enjoy very much.

Tomorrow I shall think again on my sins — which now include GLUTTONY — and how best to atone for them.

Segovia —7th of April 1466

Now that Lent is over, I can play once again upon my cittern. Forbidden to make music for the past forty days, my fingers are clumsy and the strings are out of tune. But soon I shall coax a sweet melody from it again. Made of rosewood and inlaid with ivory and gold, it once belonged to my mother. She gave it to me the last time we were together. I remember how beautifully she used to play it for my brother and me.

Segovia — 8th of April 1466

Two weeks since my conversation with Queen Juana about my "pretty summer wedding." I wait in a most anxious state for word of the betrothal. Have the *grandes* given their consent? Or is it still possible that I might escape this ill fortune?

I know that oftentimes, the bride does not set eyes upon the bridegroom before her wedding day. My mother had never seen my father before they were wed — the betrothal ceremony was carried out with ambassadors representing both bride and groom. My mother was only a little older than I when she bade her parents farewell and left Portugal with her royal attendants for her journey to Castilla and her marriage to my father. And as Queen

Juana so boldly pointed out, he was much older than my mother.

Yet she did come to love him. Since his death she has never stopped grieving for him. I do not for one moment believe that my mother enjoyed Queen Juana's notion of a "merry life" as the wife of an aged king.

"It is the duty of the woman to marry the man chosen for her," Clara has reminded me. "Others decide your destiny for you, Doña Isabel. If you are lucky, your husband will be kind, and you will learn to feel affection for him."

"But what of love, Clara?" I asked her, for I have read of such things.

"Respect is more important," is all that she will say. She presses her lips together and squints nearsightedly at her needlework.

Segovia — 9th of April 1466

I wish that, like my mother, I had never seen the man who has been chosen to be my husband. Then I could still dream of happiness. But I have seen him, two years ago when I traveled to Portugal with Enrique and Queen

Juana. From the first moment, I found him impossible to bear — the hawk's nose, the soft chin, the pale eyes set too close together. El Escorpión seems as lewd and greedy as his sister. Love will not happen between us, I am certain of that. Nor respect, either.

Still, I did much like his country when we visited. Perhaps I liked it because my mother is Portuguese and the language is familiar to me. Also because Portugal lies by the Ocean Sea.

One evening I stood by the water's edge and gazed toward the setting sun. The vastness of the sea stretched far beyond my imagining. Foaming waves crashed on the shore, and the color of the water seemed to change from blue to green to gray. As the sun sank, the sea itself disappeared into nothingness.

Later, when I spoke of my love for the sea, El Escorpión made me a gift of a little wooden ship with linen sails. It is a replica of the vessel in which his uncle, the navigator Dom Henrique, explored the coast of Africa, bringing back gold and slaves.

"They say there are lands beyond the Ocean Sea where no ship has yet sailed, inhabited by people the likes of which we have never seen," said El Escorpión.

I like to imagine it is so. I treasure the gift, much as I dislike the giver.

Segovia — 10th of April 1466

Ominously quiet. My birthday falls in less than two weeks. Surely by then I will know my fate.

Meanwhile, I am surrounded by my ladies-in-waiting, who flutter their fans and twitter like birds. They are much taken up with trying to divine their futures, which for them mean husbands and children and castles of their own.

María has a divining book with a thread dangling from each page. The ladies take turns pulling on one of the threads, opening to that page, and reading the fortune written there. Now Mencia sulks because she does not like the fortune she read, Jimena says it is better to cast dots of ink from a pen and interpret their meaning, and Elvira scorns all of it. For once I agree with Elvira. I took part, nevertheless, and learned that I shall produce five children. No hint who the father shall be.

Catalina sometimes steals off with me to the palace library to spend a quiet hour with those books that Padre Torquemada permits us to read. Today we fell to examining a chart that shows not only the towns and cities of the Kingdom of Castilla, but also the kingdoms and principalities surrounding it.

Catalina has an unusual way of seeing things. "Our peninsula is like a fist on the arm of Europe," she says, "thrust westward into the Ocean Sea. And the largest part of the fist, its greatest strength, is the Kingdom of Castilla and León."

To the northeast lies the Kingdom of Aragón. It shares its northern border with France, and its long coastline looks eastward on the Mediterranean Sea.

To the south is Granada, held by the Moors, the Muslim infidels from the northern shores of Africa. They wrested it from our Christian people more than 750 years ago. It is King Enrique's sworn duty to drive out the Moors and reclaim the land.

And then to the west, Portugal. With my finger I traced

the outline of the kingdom that, unless God intervenes, will become my home when I am the wife of El Escorpión.

I have begged Catalina to come with me if I must go to Portugal, but she shakes her head and insists that it is the convent for her.

Segovia — 12th of April 1466

After Mass this morning, I climbed the narrow, winding stone steps to a window high in one of the castle turrets. I often come up here to see what lies beyond my prison. Segovia is surrounded by four thick walls, each with a heavy wooden gate. The aqueduct built by the Romans more than a thousand years ago stretches to the horizon.

Far below the castle, the Eresma River rushes through a narrow gorge. Across the river, flocks of sheep seem to flow like a river themselves. The sheep bleat, their bells tinkle — I know this, even if I cannot hear them. In the fields beyond the walls, little green shoots of wheat are pushing up. How I yearn to be <u>there</u> instead of <u>here</u>.

When I came down, I thought I heard music coming from my chamber, and there I discovered Ana, plucking at my cittern! I was shocked, of course, and angry. A servant with my cittern! She burst into tears and fell on her knees, begging my forgiveness, which I granted. I sent the girl away and played a melancholy tune, thinking of my mother.

Segovia — 13th of April 1466

The royal seamstresses appeared in my chambers, sent by Queen Juana. I am to have several new gowns, new under-skirts and jackets and capes, all to take with me to my marriage. The seamstresses are in a fever to have every-thing ready "in time." They do not say in time for what, but that is not hard to figure out.

Queen Juana insists that my breasts be pushed up to make them seem larger, and my waist drawn in so tight that I can scarcely breathe, to make it seem smaller. For my part, I demand that the necklines come up to my chin. Truth be told, I would rather present myself to El Escorpión stitched in a grain sack.

I cannot believe the manner in which God has chosen to punish me. I know that I am wicked. I confess that I am guilty of most of the grievous sins. But surely I do not deserve what is about to happen.

The first sign of danger was the unexpected arrival of Beltrán de la Cueva. At first I marveled at my brother's favorite adviser coming here. I thought he must be calling upon Queen Juana. This would have been an occasion for gossip — not only among my ladies, but among nearly everyone else in the castle as well.

But I soon learned that Cueva had come to see me. I received him in the larger of my chambers — with Clara present, and Catalina as well. (I suspect that Ana was idling somewhere nearby.) He was, as always, dressed in velvet and furs with jeweled rings on every finger. He swept off his plumed hat and handed me a letter from King Enrique.

About El Escorpión, I thought. I broke the wax seal and opened it, noticing as I did that Cueva shifted from one elegantly booted foot to the other and stroked his silky, perfumed mustache. I prepared myself to see that the date of the betrothal had been set.

The letter was brief. King Enrique never bothers with pleasantries but goes straight to the point. I read, "You will not marry King Afonso of Portugal."

Not marry El Escorpión after all! What wonderful news!

But then my eye fell upon the next line: "It is my wish that you marry Pedro Girón."

"Pedro Girón!" I gasped, feeling my strength leave me. "This cannot be!" And I fell down in a faint.

Clara and Catalina rushed to attend me. When my eyes opened again, Clara had picked up the letter that had dropped from my hand and was reading it. Cueva, assured that I was not dead, put on his hat and departed, plumes waving. Clara began to weep.

"Your brother has ordered us to leave for Madrid at once," she said between sobs. "The wedding is to take place there in a week's time."

"But why?" I cried. "Why Girón?"

Clara shrugged helplessly. "Because the King wills it," she said.

"He must go first to the *grandes* and get their approval,"

I said, grasping at any shred of hope. "I will go and plead with them myself. Surely they will support me."

"Too late, too late!" Clara said, tears streaming down her cheeks. "The *grandes* have already given their consent. It is here, in the letter."

I seized the letter and read it all the way through. Girón is the brother of Juan Pacheco — El Zorro proposed the union! Even my faithful friend Archbishop Carrillo has agreed.

I am trapped. There is no way out.

Segovia — 15th of April 1466

I have sent a message to Beatríz, begging her to come to my aid at once. She is wise and experienced. She will know what to do.

While I wait for Beatríz, I pray — hours on my knees in the chapel, Catalina by my side, begging God's mercy. Does He hear our prayers?

Now I regret that I did not agree at once to marry El Escorpión. I should have told Queen Juana that I was pleased to be pledged to her brother. El Escorpión is thirty-three and ugly, but compared with Pedro Girón, he is almost a desirable husband. Girón is much older than El Escorpión — he is forty-three! He is even uglier, cruder, and more foul-mouthed and corrupt. Does my brother care nothing for me, to force this wretched man upon me?

I have made a vow to Santa Engracia, to whom I turn in times of severest trouble. I promised to make a pilgrimage to her shrine in Zaragoza in Aragón if she will help save me from this dreadful union.

Engracia was martyred by the Romans in the fourth century. Catalina says Engracia was a Portuguese princess, passing through Aragón on her way to her wedding in France. In Zaragoza she denounced the worship of idols that she witnessed in that city. That is why the Romans killed her by driving a spike through her head.

Engracia's skull with the hole from the spike is a precious relic kept at the Benedictine convent in Zaragoza. I will crawl on my knees to her shrine if only she will help me. Catalina has pledged to go with me.

Segovia — 16th of April 1466

Queen Juana is in a rage. She is furious at Enrique, even more than I am. All her plans for my pretty summer wedding to her brother have come to nothing! Nevertheless, this morning she came to offer me one of her gowns for my wedding to Girón. There is no time to finish the gowns on which her seamstresses have been stitching so diligently.

"This blue brocade would set off your eyes and fair skin," she said, and one of her maids held it up.

"I would rather wear a burial shroud!" I told her. She reminded me, again, that I am an ungrateful girl.

Segovia — 17th of April 1466

Beatríz has come. She explained why I am being forced into this awful marriage. She says it is to bring peace to the Kingdom.

The countryside is being torn apart by *grandes* fighting among themselves. Some support my brother King Enrique, and others support my brother Alfonso as their king. As a result the Kingdom is in turmoil. Crime is on the rise. Danger lurks everywhere. No one is safe. The peasant cannot work in the fields, and the merchant is afraid to sell his goods in the villages.

"To force the *grandes* to stop fighting," Beatríz said, "Enrique needs men and money. Pedro Girón has pledged three thousand lancers on horseback and sixty thousand gold pieces to help him. All that in exchange for marrying you."

"And my brother has agreed?" I wailed.

Beatríz nodded. I threw myself into her arms, sobbing. "What shall I do?"

"Do not fear — I have a plan," Beatríz whispered. "Look."

She opened the sleeve of her cloak and showed me a silver dagger hidden in a fold of cloth. "God will not permit this evil," she hissed, "and neither will I!"

"But what do you plan to do?" I asked, shivering.

"As Girón approaches you, I will plunge this dagger —!"

"Beatríz, no!" I cried before she could finish.

I was stunned. How could she do this? I could not let her take the life of another, or risk her own life and her immortal soul to save mine. I embraced her. "You will not have to do this," I said. "I made a vow to Santa Engracia. She will help us."

I have written to Enrique, promising in the future to be the most obedient of sisters, if he will only spare me now.

Madrid — 18th of April 1466

Late this afternoon we arrived at the royal palace in Madrid. I am accompanied by faithful Clara, fiery Beatríz, who remains determined to use her dagger to defend me, pious Catalina, who prays ceaselessly to Santa Engracia, and my other attendants. Blanca chatters with excitement, and María is thrilled to have an occasion to wear one of her new gowns! Ana has come, too. She has never been to Madrid and is wide-eyed with wonder. I am sick at heart.

I hope for an opportunity to speak to my brother, to plead with him, but so far he has not acknowledged my letter and refuses to see me.

Just after sunset, a messenger galloped in from Toledo, where Girón and his army are spending the night. They will arrive here tomorrow.

I have less than twenty-four hours.

"Please, Doña Isabel, do not worry," Beatríz says over and over, her eyes bright with determination.

But I think of the dagger in her sleeve, and of the danger, and I worry more than ever. Catalina is calm, placing her faith in Santa Engracia. Clara wrings her hands and urges me to eat, but I have vowed that not a morsel of food shall pass my lips until I am delivered from this terrible fate.

Madrid — 19th of April 1466

No word from Enrique, but there is also no word from Girón. My empty stomach rumbles. I pray and pray.

Madrid — 20th of April 1466

A day has passed, and there is still no sign of Girón. I am weak and dizzy from lack of food. In my chamber over-looking the courtyard, I can hear the clatter of the delivery carts and the cheerful voices of the cooks as they prepare my wedding feast. I want to shout down to them that they are cooking a meal for a bride who will not be alive to eat it.

But where is Girón?

Clara stays by my side, comforting as much as she can. Catalina prays on and on. But Beatríz is restless. An hour ago she went to seek word of the whereabouts of Girón. Back she came with another messenger, a frightened young fellow with a strange tale to tell:

Yesterday as Girón and his *caballeros* left Toledo, they noticed a flock of storks circling overhead. So many birds that the sky grew dark with them!

The storks seemed to be flying north, in the same direction that Girón and his men were traveling. But when a soldier pointed this out to one of the captains, the officer commanded him to be silent.

Everyone believed that the storks were an ill omen, a portent of doom. The men were terrified. Many wanted to turn back. Girón was determined to continue the journey but sent this messenger on ahead to inform King Enrique of the strange event.

"It signifies my doom," I said tearfully when Beatríz had thanked the messenger and sent him away.

"No, Doña Isabel," she insisted. "Not yours."

Madrid — 21st of April 1466

Girón is dead!

At first I was too shocked to utter a word, but Beatríz's

eyes gleamed as a new messenger brought the news: Hours after the storks filled the sky with their dire warning, Pedro Girón fell ill of the quinsy, suffering greatly from the pain in his throat. He died this morning. Now he is past his suffering, and so am I!

We are preparing to return to Segovia. I expect there will be another message from El León of another betrothal to El Escorpión. Queen Juana will again take up her plans for a pretty summer wedding. Her seamstresses will resume their work on my gowns. Blanca can squawk and Jimena gorge herself and Elvira boast all she wants, but for now — if only for now — <u>I am saved</u>!

Madrid — 22nd of April 1466

Today is my fifteenth birthday, observed this morning by a special Mass and blessing by the priest. There is no celebration, and none had been planned. King Enrique was not present. I have seen nothing of him. I am still shaken by the death of Juan Girón. I wonder what my future holds, but I do not intend to seek answers from María's divining book.

Rumors swirl around us like smoke. Perhaps Girón's

death was not because of a dreadful illness sent by God but because of poison. But who poisoned him? A man of his reputation has many enemies. If the rumor is true, then surely it was the hand of God that guided the hand of the poisoner.

Segovia — 23rd of April 1466

The only good thing about my journey to Madrid was that I could at last leave Segovia, if only for a few days. The first time in more than a year!

The weather was clear the day we left for Madrid, but my heart was stormy then, and I took no pleasure in it. Today on the return trip to Segovia I was in a mood to enjoy myself, but the weather turned foul. Even so, once we were through the mountains and on level plain, I threw back the hood of my cloak. I wanted to feel the wind and rain on my face. Clara disapproved, I know, but said nothing. By the time we reached the castle, I was soaked to the skin.

Segovia — 24th of April 1466

I have confessed to Padre Torquemada my unseemly joy at the sudden death of Pedro Girón. The priest lectured me on the sin of PRIDE (again!) and asked if I am using this book to meditate upon my sins. I told him that I use it faithfully. I did <u>not</u> tell him that my meditations are on many other subjects besides sin.

The penance he gave me is very mild — prayers only. I suspect that Torquemada is as relieved as I am at the outcome of my near-betrothal.

Segovia — 25th of April 1466

Our life here has returned to normal: I arise at dawn and say my morning prayers, dress, attend Mass in the chapel, and then join my ladies for needlework and gossip. I retire to my chamber to read the Bible and practice upon my cittern, come out to eat my dinner, and walk the castle grounds if the weather is fine (today it is not).

If Princess Juana insists, I spend time with her (her needlework shows improvement), and afterward, I write in this book. Then I sup with my ladies, say my evening prayers, and retire for the night. And so it goes, day by day, unless the routine is broken by a visitor, such as my dear Beatríz.

Beatríz (and her dagger!) left today for Arévalo, where she is to carry my most loving greetings to my mother. How I wish that I could deliver these words myself! I have not seen the Queen Widow for more than a year, and I worry about her constantly.

After Beatríz had gone, Clara confided a secret: "Many years ago, just after the death of your father, the Queen Widow received an unwelcome visitor. It was Juan Girón. Her grief was still fresh, her mourning had only begun, but he had come to propose marriage. She was weeping when she told me of their conversation."

"Naturally, she refused him," I said.

"Naturally. But his proposal insulted her. It is my belief," Clara continued, "that your mother's current unhappy condition began with Girón's insult."

I have long wondered at the circumstances that brought about my mother's madness. I love her deeply, with all the strength of a daughter's heart. Yet I know that something is terribly wrong.

Even when I was a child, and my brother Alfonso was

still too young to notice, our mother would sit for hours, gazing at nothing. Not hearing when I spoke to her, not seeing when my brother reached up his arms to her. Sometimes for days she uttered not a word. And when she did speak, it was to cry out that Arévalo was haunted, that the river flowing nearby whispered her name night and day. Had Girón caused this collapse?

"Girón is a beast," I agreed. Then I corrected myself. "He <u>was</u> a beast. He will insult women no longer."

Segovia — 26th of April 1466

My head aches, my face is flushed and hot, and I think I shall lie down.

Segovia — 27th of April 1466

Chills and fever. Clara called for the royal physician. He diagnosed ague. I have no strength to write.

Today is the first time in more than a week that I have felt well enough to write. I remember scarcely anything of the past days except my body shaking with chills and a burning fever that brought on strange visions: Once again I heard Ana playing my cittern, and when I cried out to her to stop, she said it was my mother's wish for her to heal me with music. Later, when I told Clara, she said I had dreamed it all.

Doctor Abravanel came to my chamber each day to bleed me, cutting a vein in my arm and letting the blood flow to remove impurities.

Now that I am better, he has prescribed a mixture of white onion with vinegar and oregano, and a tea brewed of borage and sow thistle. It is almost too bitter to swallow, but Clara makes sure that I do. She blames my illness on my ride in the rain but has the kindness not to lecture me on my lack of good sense.

Catalina sits patiently by my bedside, hour after hour, stitching on her banner. She is nearly finished with the Lamb and will soon begin to work on its golden crown to be set with real pearls.

We have discussed plans for our pilgrimage to Zaragoza, when I am strong again and when (if!) Enrique decides to allow me to leave Segovia. It is quite a long journey to Zaragoza, in the Kingdom of Aragón — perhaps seven or eight days in a litter carried by mules. I am most interested in seeing Santa Engracia's skull with the hole made by the spike.

Segovia — 9th of May 1466

Doctor Abravanel has pronounced me cured, although I am still quite weak.

Like most physicians the doctor is a Jew. Jews do seem to have special talent in the art of healing. Does their religion somehow make it so? I also wonder why the doctor's family did not convert generations ago, as Catalina's did.

"Why does Doctor Abravanel insist upon remaining a Jew," I asked Catalina, "and upon living in a ghetto and wearing a yellow badge? Why does not everyone convert? I am surprised that a single Jew remains in all of Castilla, when it is so much easier to be a Christian."

Catalina sighed. "I have no idea. It must be very important to them to remain Jewish. My family has been

Christian since the conversions a century ago," she told me. "After the Black Death, my great-grandfather understood that it was much, much better to be a Christian, and he and the whole Valera family converted. And so we have remained pious Christians to this day."

I did not mention to Catalina that many Old Christians still mistrust the *conversos*, as we call the Jewish converts to Christianity. Some people believe the *conversos* still practice their Jewish ways in secret. But there were questions I wanted to put to Catalina.

I said, "Some say many Jews were killed because people believed they stole Christian children to use in their rituals. Others claim the Jews poisoned the wells, and that they could call forth the Devil. Do you believe that?"

"No," Catalina insisted. "I do not."

"They are also said to be avid for money — and it is true that Jews collect the taxes and lend money. Why is this, then?"

Catalina's dark head was bent over some part of the Lamb's hoof on which she was working. She did not look at me as she replied, "Jews are the moneylenders because Christians are forbidden to lend money."

And our conversation ended there.

Later

I am still thinking about the Jewish question.

I know that Jews have been blamed for causing the Black Death to spread, which is hard to believe since Jews as well as Christians died of the plague. As punishment, many Jews were put to death. The rest were not allowed to be addressed with titles of respect, such as *Don* or *Doña*. There were other rules, too: Jews were not permitted to wear rich clothing, and they had to live in *aljamas,* separate from Christians. Was it not better to convert? Was it not easier?

Last winter Padre Torquemada preached a sermon in which he claimed that no *converso* could be trusted to be a sincere Christian. "Their blood is forever tainted," Torquemada thundered. Catalina was sitting near me with her family that Sunday. I remember wondering how they felt when the royal chapel rang with the priest's harsh words: <u>forever tainted</u>.

Since then I have heard whispered remarks about the Valera family. I always thought those cruel remarks resulted from jealousy of her father's position. But now I sometimes wonder: Is Catalina one of those *conversos* who still light candles on Friday nights as though it were the

Sabbath? Who recite their prayers in Hebrew? Could it be that my dear Catalina, who prays so fervently to Santa Engracia, is secretly a Jew?

Segovia — 16th of May 1466

Last night, after everyone else had gone to sleep, I took a lighted candle and climbed the winding stairs of the turret. From a small window near the top, I gazed up at the great bowl of the heavens and watched the slow circling dance of moon and stars and planets.

Only two days ago, I confessed to Padre Torquemada that I am guilty of the sin of ENVY — envy of my own younger brother, whose education is so much more interesting than mine, which ceased at the age of twelve. Alfonso is being tutored as a *caballero*, a knight, whereas I was taught only reading, writing, and ciphering and more than a dozen embroidery stitches!

But it is not knighthood that interests me. It is the study of the stars and planets. I have heard that the great navigators read the stars to steer their ships. Imagine being out on the Ocean Sea, far from any shore, yet able to reckon the position of the ship by studying the heavens!

"I should love to have such knowledge," I admitted to Padre Torquemada.

At once he began to lecture me sternly. "Doña Isabel," he began in that voice from a deep, dark place, "please understand this: Woman is inferior, because that is how God created her. It was Eve's frailty that caused her to tempt Adam with the Fruit of the Tree in the Garden of Eden. As a result of Eve's sin, she and Adam were driven out of Paradise. Hers is the weakness of all women."

Weakness, indeed! *Clearly*, I thought, *he does not know Beatríz de Bobadilla, with the dagger hidden in her cloak.*

"But Padre," I said, "what has Eve's sin to do with the study of the stars?"

The priest narrowed his eyes and peered down his sharp nose at me. "Eve's sin has shown that it is the duty of man to protect women from temptation. To allow women to study astronomy and mathematics and those other subjects that you find so tempting" — here he smiled, a smile as thin and cold as the blade of a sword — "would only weaken their frail natures. It would lead them from their natural purity into darkest sin."

Then he gave me a book that he deems fit for me: *Garden of Noble Maidens*, written by a friar of the Order of

Saint Augustine. I have read the first chapters and agree there is no chance this book will lead me astray. I have twice fallen asleep over its dull pages.

Segovia — 18th of May 1466

The Augustinian friar has much to say about chastity, modesty, a sense of shame, and a guarded tongue. To support all of this, he goes on for pages about how Eve was created from Adam's rib. He even claims to know exactly which rib!

Segovia — 21st of May 1466

The weather is fine, and my ladies and I amused ourselves with a stroll to the Plaza Mayor, the main square. Even a short walk is hard for Catalina, whose leg hurts her after only a few steps. Still, she insists on accompanying me with her odd, dipping gait.

Although I am permitted to leave the castle without an escort, Enrique manages through his spies to keep one eye on me at all times, like a sleepy lion. I dare not rouse El León, lest he begin roaring again about a betrothal to El

Escorpión. A pilgrimage to Zaragoza seems out of the question for now.

We managed to walk as far as the Convent of San Francisco, where the nuns greeted us warmly and fed us sweet cakes (greatly pleasing Jimena, who had three of everything) and sent us on our way again.

Segovia — 24th of May 1466

I can think of nothing to write. My current life is tiresome and drab while I wait for El León to awaken and decide my future.

Segovia — 25th of May 1466

To amuse me, Catalina has offered to teach me to draw. I am not an apt pupil, as we soon discovered. For our first lesson, she had me sketch an orange on a plate. When I rendered it as a crooked circle balanced on a more-or-less straight line, she shook her head. I want to draw sheep and mules and peasants in the fields, but she tells me, very respectfully, that I am a long way from such an undertaking.

Segovia — 29th of May 1466

Another new enterprise: I have decided to give Ana lessons on the cittern. Clara disapproves of this, because Ana is not of a noble family and is a servant (an eager but clumsy one, it must be said). Yet I am unable to forget the feverish dream in which Ana appeared to me, plucking the strings and assuring me that my mother wished it.

Her gratitude is touching. More surprising, though, is her talent. I suspect that she has more than I do.

Segovia — 30th of May 1466

Another surprise: Ana has a voice like a nightingale. I must be careful, lest I commit (again!) the sin of ENVY.

Segovia — 5th of June 1466
The Feast of Corpus Christi

It was Queen Juana's idea to celebrate this religious festival. "Come, Doña Isabel, you are young!" she cried. "Enjoy yourself while you can!"

And I thought, *She is right. Soon I will no doubt be married to her brother.*

I changed into my favorite gown, wine-colored velvet, with a cloak of deep blue. But of course I did not nearly match the finery of Queen Juana. She was stuffed into a whalebone corset, her green brocade sleeves puffed up as big as melons, and she tottered along in clogs with painted soles so thick that she appeared to have grown half a head taller. A young girl carried her train, and the Queen herself had only to flutter her perfumed peacock whisk. I trailed behind with my small suite, including Catalina.

Naturally, Enrique did not join us. "He is with his animals, as usual," Queen Juana informed us.

We made our way to one of the grand houses on the Plaza Mayor belonging to friends of the Queen. From our places on the balcony, we had a fine view of the procession passing below us.

First came the priests in shimmering robes of embroidered silk, followed by the monks in their plain habits made of rough-woven cloth. After them rode the *grandes* of Segovia — Catalina's father among them. The horses were dressed nearly as well as their riders. All were escorting a jeweled chest containing the Host, the consecrated bread that is the Body of Christ. That was the solemn part of the procession.

Next, leaping and shouting, came the crowd of fools and jesters dressed in motley, their multicolored clothing and belled caps. The giants and the big-headed dwarfs, towering figures made of papier-mâché, whirled by, gesturing up at us. Terrified, little Princess Juana clung whimpering to her mother's skirts until the Queen impatiently brushed her aside.

Just then *La Tarasca*, the wooden dragon, made its fearful appearance. With its enormous belly and long tail covered in scales, it was pulled along on wheels. Rolling its fearsome eyes and opening its great painted jaws to show off three tongues and row upon row of fangs, *La Tarasca* uttered horrible moans and yells. The dragon sent poor Princess Juana into a fit of anguished weeping, and she hurled herself at me.

I knelt down and gathered the frightened child close to me. Her mother was too busy laughing and calling out to her friends to pay any attention, and the child's nursemaid was nowhere to be seen.

Later

After the sun went down and the torches were lighted, Queen Juana and her friends appeared in elaborate disguises. "You must come with us, Doña Isabel!" Queen Juana called out, but I knew that she expected me to refuse. And I did.

With her little daughter asleep on my lap, I watched from the balcony as the Queen descended to the street and entered a waiting carriage with two of her ladies-in-waiting. The Plaza Mayor, which earlier had been crowded with religious and carnival figures, now swirled with revelers. The night was filled with the sounds of guitars and flutes and jingling tambourines. Soon the dancing would begin.

Young dandies sauntered around the Plaza Mayor, wearing close-fitting doublets over whalebone frames to broaden their chests, and padded stockings to give themselves more shapely legs. Elaborate linen ruffs made their heads look like a cheese on a plate. Like the ladies, they were masked.

One of the men boldly tossed an eggshell filled with perfumed water into the Queen's carriage. I heard my sister-in-law's shrill laughter and saw her silk-gloved hand reach out to touch his cheek.

I leaned forward to get a better look at the eggshell thrower. At that moment he glanced up at the balcony where I sat holding the sleeping Princess. Our eyes met. It was Beltrán de la Cueva.

Segovia — 6th of June 1466

Catalina and I worked on our sketches for nearly an hour today. I attempted to draw *La Tarasca*, but the dragon was well beyond my skills. Then I settled down to sketching one of the Venetian glass goblets that Queen Juana so highly prizes. It is the most lovely shade of blue. My drawing looks as though the goblet is made of melting wax. Catalina's is elegant.

While we were bent over our paper and pens, Catalina murmured, "You know, do you not, that Andrés de Cabrera is a New Christian?"

"Of course," I said, my eyes on my pen. But in truth I had forgotten that the man Beatríz will marry is of *converso* descent.

"Does it matter to you?"

"Not if he is a sincere Christian."

Catalina said nothing more, and neither did I. But the words of Padre Torquemada's sermon echoed in my head: <u>forever tainted.</u>

Segovia — 7th of June 1466

A most welcome visit from Beatríz, who surprised us with her arrival yesterday from Arévalo. This is the first I have seen her since the death of Pedro Girón. She is fairly bursting with cheer, full of plans for her wedding in September.

When she asked for news since we were last together in Madrid, I told her of my illness and described the Corpus Christi festival.

"And El Escorpión? Enrique says nothing about a betrothal?" she asked.

The mere mention of him always makes me feel ill. "Nothing," I said. "And I ask nothing. I just pray that another suitor will appear from somewhere before it is too late."

"Yes, dear Isabel," she said. "I pray daily that you will be granted a husband as fine as my Andrés."

But not a converso, I thought.

Segovia — 8th of June 1466

This morning I showed Beatríz the book Padre Torquemada has me read. She made a face.

"The castle library is filled with much more interesting books," she said briskly. "You must read whatever you wish."

It is true that there are shelves of books, hundreds of volumes, and I sometimes walk up and down, choosing a book and then hurriedly putting it back.

"But is it not a sin for me to read them?" I asked Beatríz, somewhat shocked. Beatríz is always shocking me. That is one of the reasons I like her so much.

She frowned at me, her hands propped on her hips. "Only if you believe it to be," she said. "Are you still writing all your so-called sins in that book Torquemada gave you?"

I admitted that I was.

Beatríz clicked her tongue, *tsk, tsk*. "You must make me a promise: that you will no longer record your sins but only your joys. Your life has become too gloomy. I wish better for you, Doña Isabel."

Now I was completely aghast. I cannot imagine defying

Padre Torquemada, who always convinces me that I can actually feel the heat of the Eternal Flames.

Segovia — 10th of June 1466

Before she left today to return to Arévalo, Beatríz proposed an exciting idea: that we go to the annual trade fair at Medina del Campo next month. "You can come to Arévalo and have a visit with your mother. Then we will ride on to the fair."

"Enrique will never permit it," I complained. I was truly unhappy, because I used to go every year to the fair with Alfonso, and I long to go again.

"Then we must find a way to persuade him. Perhaps he will consent if you travel with a company of his *caballeros*. And it would be safer that way. I will write to him. Leave it all to me."

So I allow myself to dream of it, but I am not truly hopeful. I have not heard from El León — not a single word — since the death of Girón. I dread that when I do, it will not be to grant permission to go to the fair but to announce the beginning of my miserable life with El Escorpión.

Segovia — 23rd of June 1466

We are going to the fair! King Enrique has consented, and in ten days we leave. It is not exactly as I wished it to be, for Queen Juana and Princess Juana will be in our party, and all of their attendants and mine, plus a number of knights to guard us. Still!

Even Catalina is excited.

Segovia — 27th of June 1466

Enrique has changed his mind. Not completely — just half. I am not to visit my mother. He has decided that instead of traveling to Medina del Campo by way of Arévalo, we are instead to go by way of Coca and spend the night at the castle belonging to his friend Bishop Fonseca. Enrique gives no explanation for this. No sense asking for one.

Segovia — 29th of June 1466

The journey has been canceled. Again, no explanation. I am not the only one who is upset — Queen Juana is absolutely furious! The woman has a temper beyond measure. She seized everything within reach and threw it at the wall.

The silver is dented, the French porcelain shattered, the Venetian glass goblets smashed to bits. It was quite a sight.

Beatríz is right: I am so gloomy that I hardly know what to do with myself. I am tired of my own complaints and have nothing more that I wish to write about. If ever the dull monotony is altered, I shall resume writing.

Segovia — 22nd of April 1467

Today is my sixteenth birthday. For ten months I have not recorded my thoughts, having had little reason to do so. But Beatríz came to share the day with me (she brought me a set of silver combs as a gift) and urged me to begin again. "My wish is that you write of joyous things, and few sorrows," she said.

This would not be difficult were I Beatríz. My dear friend was married last September. I have never seen a bride more radiant, or a new husband more delighted with his wife! At the time of her wedding, Beatríz promised me that her marriage would not interfere with our friendship, and thus far she has kept her promise.

Since then she has come here several times, when Andrés is elsewhere with King Enrique. She glows with happiness, and I try to banish my envious feelings. (Otherwise I shall have to return to recording my sins.)

We were walking together in the courtyard when once again Beatríz brought up the subject of my suitor — or lack thereof. "Is there any news of a betrothal?" she asked, as she asks during every visit.

"None," I told her. "Enrique says nothing, and neither do I. He seems to have forgotten about it."

She smiled at me, her delicate eyebrows arched. "I suspect that your prayers will soon be answered," she said.

I halted our walk and clutched her arm. "You suspect? Suspect what? What do you mean, Doña Beatríz?"

"Nothing, Doña Isabel," she assured me, patting my hand. "Nothing at all."

"I do not believe you!" I cried. "Have you heard something? You must tell me!"

"I have heard nothing," she said serenely. "But your prayers have been answered in the past, have they not? And you must believe that they will be again."

Everything is more interesting when Beatríz is here. Each time she leaves, I miss her for days.

Segovia — 25th of April 1467

More than a year has passed since the death of Girón, but Catalina and I have not yet made our pilgrimage to the shrine of Santa Engracia. Catalina has long since completed her banner of the Lamb of God, and finished two others as well. I have sewn more shirts than Alfonso can possibly wear out.

But our drawing lessons continue: I have discovered a small talent for capturing the details of buildings, especially the graceful archways and intricate ironwork of Moorish design. The drawing is a distraction. So are Ana's music lessons. Now if only I could teach her to keep the candlewicks trimmed!

Segovia — 26th of May 1467

I have resolved that I shall go into the town at every opportunity when the weather is fine with a sheet of parchment and my pens and ink, and will draw some scene that strikes my eye.

Today I began work on a drawing of the aqueduct. The two tiers of arches — there are said to be 163 of them, but

I did not count — stretch as far as I can see. They offer a challenge to my eye and to my pen.

Catalina warns me that I have undertaken an enormous challenge and must not be disappointed if the results do not meet my expectations.

Segovia — 2nd of June 1467

Catalina was right. For the past week, I have gone out every day, save Sunday, to study and sketch the aqueduct. The results are not only disappointing but dismal.

She says I spend too much time on the details in the beginning. To illustrate, she took my pen from my hand, turned over a sad drawing that I had already tossed aside in a temper, and with a few gracefully curving lines, managed to capture the grand sweep of the ancient stone arches.

I did not feel like trying after I had seen what she could do, and my ladies and I gathered our things and returned to the castle.

Segovia — 8th of June 1467

Clara has received word through her husband, Gonzalo Chacón, that the rebel forces supporting my brother Alfonso are gaining strength. In the middle of it is our cherished friend Archbishop Carrillo.

It seems that one day, the *grandes* and the bishops favor King Alfonso, and the next day or the next week, they shift their loyalty to King Enrique. But now, according to Chacón, Carrillo has persuaded the most powerful *grandes* — those with the biggest armies — to rally behind my younger brother. The Archbishop, who maintains a huge private army of his own, believes that Alfonso will be a better king than Enrique.

I agree, but I try to balance in the middle, outwardly favoring neither one nor the other. I have no idea how this will affect me.

Segovia — 10th of June 1467

Catalina reminds me that it was my father's idea to make this old castle, built four hundred years ago, into a royal residence. "The castle is beautiful," she says. "It is a fit subject for your pen and paper, Doña Isabel."

She is right. The castle is beautiful. It is because I cannot leave it that I see it only as a prison. Following her advice, I have decided to practice, rendering the castle in parts — the wooden drawbridge, for example, and the azure turrets, and the magnificent central tower. When my drawings improve, perhaps I shall copy them into this book. Then, when I am gone from here, I shall not forget the place where I passed the years of my young womanhood. But first, let me be gone!

No further news about Alfonso and the rebels.

Segovia — 13th of June 1467

A bad idea. I shall never have the talent to render suitable drawings of this or any other place. Catalina scolds me for lack of patience. I tell her that she must be the one who draws the pictures, and that I shall content myself with words.

It must be said: Ana's playing improves each day.

Arévalo — 17th of June 1467

<u>I am free!</u>

The events of the last few days are nearly unbelievable. Not only am I liberated from the tyranny of King Enrique and Queen Juana, but here I am at home once more in Arévalo.

It all happened this way:

Last night, after we had retired, Clara and I were awakened by a commotion in the courtyard. We had no idea what was happening. Then we heard shouting and footsteps outside our door. Clara and I hurried to fling on our clothes and cowered in a corner, not knowing what to do. We could hear the ladies-in-waiting weeping, Blanca wailing at the top of her lungs.

Suddenly, the burly figure of Archbishop Carrillo nearly filling my doorway. He was dressed not as a priest but as a knight. He explained that his friends had left the city gates unlocked for him, and that he and his soldiers had rushed into the city and headed straight for the castle.

"Doña Isabel," said the Archbishop when I had recovered from my shock, "it is your choice. You may stay here, under my protection, or you may leave. Queen Juana has made her decision: She and her daughter have already fled to Enrique's castle in Madrid."

I had no need to think about it. "Your Grace," I said, "I wish to return to Arévalo and my Lady Mother as soon as possible."

By daybreak all of my possessions had been packed into wooden carts, and we were on our way. I made sure that I carried this book and a handful of the few poor sketches I have made. By the end of the day, our company, escorted by two hundred mounted horsemen, had reached Arévalo. Beatríz was here to greet me.

I rushed to my mother and tearfully flung my arms about her. There was no response. I stepped back and looked at her. My mother's hair, once a shining red-gold like mine, hung limply about her shoulders, and her gown was untidy. She stared at me with vacant eyes.

"It has been a long time," I said gently. "More than two years. Perhaps you do not recognize me. I am your daughter, Isabel."

But she seemed not even to see me. I took one of her hands in both of mine. It was icy cold, although the day was mild.

Beatríz touched my shoulder. "Come, Doña Isabel," she

whispered, and led me away from my mother's chamber. Thus what began as one of the happiest days of my life ended in sorrow.

Arévalo — 23rd of June 1467

I go to my mother's chamber at least twice each day. I try to talk with her, but it is as if she is made of wood. When I play the cittern, her tears flow unchecked, but still she does not speak.

Clara consoles me, as does Beatríz. "Why did you not tell me of this?" I cried, and Beatríz explained, "Because you could do nothing about it."

My brother King Alfonso will come soon for a visit. I do look forward to seeing him again. I remember how we used to run about the countryside, wading in streams to snare trout, and chasing rabbits in the fields. We never had much luck. When we pitched stones at distant tree stumps, his aim was surer. But I always rode better than he did. I wonder if he remembers these things?

Arévalo — 25th of June 1467

Alfonso was a little boy the last time I saw him. Now he is a king! He was a very serious little boy, and that has not changed. He arrived here this morning, dressed in silks and velvets and mounted on a fine white stallion. He was accompanied by the sound of blaring trumpets. Two hundred *caballeros* rode with him, wearing his colors, black and red. What excitement!

Alfonso seems completely unlike our brother Enrique in every way. Enrique prefers to ride in the Moorish style, on a small, fast horse with the stirrups shortened so that his knees are bent. Enrique dresses badly, whereas Alfonso clearly likes his finery. And Enrique has no interest in the rituals of being king. Alfonso not only enjoys these rituals but demands them!

When I ran to greet him — I have not seen him in nearly four years — I was waved back by one of his ushers with the command, "Obedience to the King! Obedience to the King!"

Surprised, I stopped and made a deep bow. Still mounted on his horse, King Alfonso motioned to me to step forward and kiss his hand, which I did.

"I am happy to see you, Doña Isabel," he said gravely.

"And I you, My Lord," I said just as gravely, although I admit I felt like laughing. He is, after all, still but a boy without a beard!

"You have become very pretty, Isabel," he said in that same formal tone, but in a boy's voice.

I bowed again. "You are most gracious, My Lord."

After this exchange of greetings, we made a grand procession to the Convent of San Francisco outside the walls of the town. There was Carrillo, no longer dressed as a knight with a silver sword but as an Archbishop carrying a jeweled cross. Arrayed in a vestment made of gold cloth embroidered from neck to hem with rich silk and precious stones, he celebrated a Mass of thanksgiving.

I kept stealing glances at Alfonso, who knelt by my side. How tall and handsome my brother is becoming, although he is not yet fourteen. And he is so sure of himself! He seems determined to be a good king.

Arévalo — 26th of June 1467

Last evening after we returned to the castle, we enjoyed a fine feast, which the servants had managed to prepare for

74

us on short notice. My poor mother did not join us, but remained shut away in her chamber.

At the banquet I sat beside King Alfonso, who regally received the greetings of many of his supporters. On the other side of me was the Archbishop. I asked about El Zorro, the Archbishop's wily nephew. The last I heard, he was on Alfonso's side.

"Pacheco is with Enrique," Carrillo replied. "He has changed sides once more."

Don Andrés is not here with Beatríz — he is in Madrid with Enrique. I can see that this puts a great strain on her, for her loyalties are divided. She is not the only one! Of my six ladies-in-waiting, only Elvira did not come with us from Segovia. Her father is loyal to Enrique.

In her stead I have invited Alicia, a niece of the Archbishop, to join my retinue of ladies. She seems pleasant company, and not nearly so vain of her intelligence as Elvira. Her worst fault is her habit of humming off-key.

Arévalo — 30th of June 1467

We are going to the trade fair at Medina del Campo! This is Alfonso's suggestion. He knows how much I enjoy it.

Last year Enrique stopped us from going, but this year he cannot.

We leave tomorrow.

Medina del Campo — 3rd *of July* 1467

Here is a short list of things for sale at the fair:
- Woolen cloth from England
- Gold-threaded satins and brocades made from silk spun in factories in Granada and North Africa
- Wool rugs and saddle blankets in intricate designs, woven by Moors
- Brasswork, including urns, lanterns, and screens, made by Moorish artisans
- Furs of all kinds: marten, beaver, fox, and sable from as far away as Russia. Ermine, too — very expensive!
- Honey
- Salt, pepper, ginger, cloves, cinnamon, and other spices brought from the Orient
- Jade and gems of all sorts, also from the Orient
- Porcelain from France and glassware from Venice (Queen Juana could replace all that she has broken)
- Many items of leather and of wood

· Powdered substances said to be from the horn of a unicorn, for what use I know not.

These are merely the things that interested me. My list does not include those items that captured Alfonso's fancy, such as helmets and brassards and shields from England, and swords from France.

Although I have little money (Enrique has never given me the rents and taxes that I am to receive from the town of Trujillo), I did make a few purchases:

· an ivory bodkin, nicely carved with roses, for Beatríz to fasten up her hair
· fine linen neckcloths for each of my ladies-in-waiting
· a bottle of cloves steeped in orange-blossom water for Clara, who complains that her skin has become rough
· a lacquered salt box for Alfonso.

As for myself, I was much taken by a Moorish bracelet of amber set in gold but had not the money for it and instead bought a crystal ink pot.

Although trade is the reason for the fair, there is much to do besides buying and bartering. Minstrels wander about, playing their citterns and flutes and bagpipes. Singers entertain with ballads. Giant figures on stilts stride through the crowds. Tumblers turn cartwheels and somersaults, and jugglers keep all sorts of objects whirling in the air above their heads.

Later, a great black bear dressed in a belled cap and a red satin jacket shambled by at the end of a golden chain. When the bear tamer began to play a tune on a little flute, the bear rose up on his hind legs and executed a slow, solemn dance.

We stopped to watch a puppet show of carved and painted figures reenacting a battle between the Moors and the Christians. The Christians won. They always do in these reenactments.

Alfonso, strolling by my side, watched as well. "Dear sister Isabel," he said, in that serious way he has, "be assured that I have vowed to drive out the Moorish invaders. As King of Castilla, I shall reclaim Christian lands from the Muslim infidels now and for all eternity."

"God will bless you," I murmured. I did not mention that if Alfonso manages to do that, he will have accomplished what no Castilian king has done in the past 750 years — including our brother Enrique.

Medina del Campo — 5th of July 1467

What a grievous lesson we learned today.

With war much on his mind, Alfonso insisted that we attend a joust. Pedro Pimentel, one of Alfonso's *caballeros*, had been challenged by a knight from Salamanca.

Pimentel, a fair-haired lad from Valladolid, entered the lists dressed in a quilted doublet of olive cut velvet with green brocade and scarlet breeches. He carried a golden sword. The challenger rode in on a fine horse caparisoned with red damask bordered with sable.

After many trumpet fanfares, the joust began. Challenger and defender moved to opposite ends of the tilting field, turned and rode toward each other at full gallop, their lances at the ready. On the first charge, the challenger struck the defender with a tremendous clash of metal, but both knights kept their seats. And so it went on each successive charge, Alfonso cheering for his *caballero*.

The day was hot, and my ladies-in-waiting fanned themselves and dabbed at their glistening faces with handkerchiefs. María and Mencia complained that they were going to perish from the heat. We were scarcely paying attention when challenger and defender began their ninth charge.

But this time the challenger from Salamanca hit Pimentel in such a way that the tip of his lance struck the boy's visor from his helmet. To the horror of all, the tip of his lance ran through the boy's eye and into his brain. Poor Pimentel fell to the ground. My ladies all turned away, covering their eyes.

The Salamancan reined in his horse and rushed to the boy's side. Alfonso leaped over the wooden barriers, shouting for a physician. Too late. Those already near the fallen knight shook their heads. Pimentel was dead.

The Salamancan knelt by the body, weeping bitterly. Pimentel's companions rushed out and returned with a Franciscan monk. I knew what the friar was saying: The Holy Church is opposed to jousting and denies the sacraments to those who die in the lists. There will be no funeral Mass for this dead *caballero*, no burial in holy ground. The monk glared sternly at Alfonso.

I felt sorry for my brother, who wept piteously for his friend. Catalina limped to my side. "I wish that boy had not died," she said, "and that if he had to die, he could be properly mourned. But he defied the law of the Church, Doña Isabel. There is no way around it."

No one, I thought, *is more obedient to the Church and to*

God's will than I am. But this converso daughter, feared to be weak in her faith, thought to be forever tainted, is more obedient than I.

Arévalo — 8th of July 1467

It was a sad company that made its way home. The death of Pedro Pimentel cast a pall of gloom over us all, especially over my brother. It may be that King Alfonso has begun to think differently about jousting.

Arévalo — 14th of July 1467

While we were at the fair, Beatríz's husband returned from Enrique's camp. Don Andrés will remain here for the rest of the month. I sometimes see the two of them walking together, smiling into each other's eyes, as though no one else in the world exists.

At times I dislike Andrés intensely. Not because of his bond with Enrique, but because of his bond with Beatríz.

We celebrated our Beatríz's feast day with a fine banquet, served in the courtyard of the castle, followed by singing and dancing. All of us wore our best gowns and jewels, but none was more beautiful than Beatríz. Even my mother allowed herself to be gowned and her hair done up for the occasion. Although she scarcely spoke at all, I did see her smile a little when the music began.

I had nearly forgotten how much I enjoy dancing — the one useful skill taught me by my "tutor," Queen Juana. I had no lack of partners and could have kept on for hours.

But I am worried about Alfonso. My brother has not been himself since the death of Pimentel.

Arévalo — 1st of August 1467

I have rarely, if ever, seen my dear friend Beatríz in tears, but yesterday she wept. "My heart is torn," she cried.

"Torn how? Between what and what?"

"Between my affection for you and my love for Andrés.

Before he left this morning to rejoin Enrique, my husband swore me to secrecy. But you are my dearest friend, and I must tell you, even though I promised him I would not."

Dear Beatríz, always taking risks for my sake! I clasped her pale hands in mine. "Tell me," I whispered.

And this is what she said: "King Juan of Aragón has sent his ambassador to Enrique with a proposal. He wants you as a wife for his son, Prince Fernando."

I squeezed her hands tightly. "Prince Fernando? What do you know of him? What did Enrique say?"

Beatríz pulled free her hand and placed her fingers on my lips. "Hush, Doña Isabel, I beg you! No one must hear of this!"

I tried to be calm. "Tell me, please, all that you know."

"I know several things. First, that King Juan is an old man, still strong but nearly blind. That he dotes on his only son, Fernando, and has granted him the title of King of Sicily. Now King Juan needs Enrique's help to keep the French from invading Aragón. And he knows that Enrique would like to have a close alliance with Aragón, with its long coast on the Mediterranean Sea. So the old King is eager to make the match."

Impatience had gotten the better of me. "But what of <u>him</u>?" I cried. "What of Fernando? Another old and ugly suitor?"

"Not old, young — just fifteen, a year younger than you. And not ugly. Andrés has met him and reports that the Prince is of medium stature, strong and well made."

"Stupid, then? Cruel?"

"Neither one, Doña Isabel," said Beatríz, smiling. "Kind and intelligent. I think him the perfect match for you."

By then I, too, was smiling. But there was still an unanswered question, the largest of all: "And what did Enrique say?"

"He is thinking it over. King Juan's ambassador is still waiting for an answer."

"Pity the poor ambassador! Enrique's greatest talent is thinking things over. His second-greatest talent is changing his mind."

"All we can do is remain hopeful," said Beatríz.

"And prayerful," I added. "Pray that my life will change soon after all."

I pray and pray, but there is no reply. No word from Enrique, who has not spoken or written to me since I left his captivity. Only this interesting piece of gossip, whispered to me by Clara: Enrique has sent Queen Juana to live in Coca at the castle of his ally Bishop Fonseca.

"It is common knowledge," says Clara, "that the Queen is happy to be apart from her husband, and he from her." Perhaps this is why he has not seen fit to write to me.

Still nothing. Archbishop Carrillo came for a few days and said Mass yesterday. After we had supped, he challenged me to a game of chess. It had been a long time since I have played with him, or with anyone else. My ladies-in-waiting do not find the game interesting.

He called for a chessboard, and we lined up our pieces on the squares of dark and light marble. I had the ivory pieces, he the ebony. We made our opening moves.

My favorite piece is the Queen, and I would have expected him to favor the Bishop. "No," he said. "It's the

Knight's moves that interest me. The Bishop is predictable, always moving on the diagonal. But the Knight moves forward and then steps aside. Like this." Suddenly his Knight captured one of my Pawns.

I glanced up at him. "I was not paying attention," I said, excusing myself.

"A mistake," he said. "You must always pay attention. An important lesson, Doña Isabel."

The game proceeded. I made a few moves that I thought clever, but in no time at all, the Archbishop had my King in check.

He patted his ample stomach and called for wine to be brought, and we talked of other things. But if Archbishop Carrillo knows anything about King Juan's proposal to Enrique, he said nothing to me.

And I dared not ask.

Arévalo — 1st of September 1467

This is Ana's feast day. She is named not for Santa Ana, the mother of the Blessed Virgin, but for another saint, a woman who saw the boy Jesus in the Temple in Jerusalem and prophesied that He would be the Redeemer of Israel. I arranged to have a special cake in honor of her day, and she was so pleased that she wept.

Arévalo — 15th of September 1467

Wonderful news from Beatríz — she expects a child in the spring. I have begun to sew again, this time tiny garments for my godchild. Alfonso says he has no need of additional shirts.

No news of Prince Fernando.

Arévalo — 1st of October 1467

I have decided not to bother our Gracious God or any of his Blessed Saints any further on the subject of the Prince of Aragón. This is the last time I will write his name in this book until I have definite word: FERNANDO.

Arévalo — 5th of November 1467

Since the sad death of Pimentel last summer, I have seen little of Alfonso. He moves about from town to town with his *caballeros*, trying to keep the support of the rebels. But in a week we shall celebrate his fourteenth birthday, and we are making plans for a reunion.

I have hired the services of a poet to write a little play in honor of the occasion. My ladies-in-waiting will play the roles of Muses, bearing gifts of virtues and skills. Catalina is to represent Intelligence. For my part, I shall enact Fortune and will remind Alfonso of the prophecy made at the time of his birth.

When Alfonso was born, our father hired an astrologer, who predicted that the stars would keep the boy's life under threat for the first fourteen years. But if Alfonso reached the age of fourteen, the stargazer promised, he would live to be the happiest prince in all of Christendom.

Arévalo — 14th of November 1467

I am not certain that my brother is the happiest prince in all of Christendom, but he did appear pleased with our little play. The performance went well, although Catalina was so nervous, she forgot the lines Intelligence was to speak. And she is the most intelligent of all my ladies! Afterward, we feasted grandly.

As a sign of our reunion and our loyalty to each other,

and in honor of my feast day tomorrow, my brother has pledged me the town of Medina del Campo. I shall now have some income from the taxes and rents. Enrique always kept me poor, but poor I am no longer!

Arévalo — 15th of November 1467
The Feast of Santa Isabel

I have always loved the saint for whom I am named — as was my mother and my mother's mother, down through seven generations. When I was a little girl, I used to beg my mother to tell me the story of Isabel, cousin of the Virgin Mary. Isabel and her husband, Zacharias, believed she was too old to bear a child. When the Angel Gabriel told Zacharias the good news that Isabel had conceived, Zacharias did not believe him, and Gabriel struck him dumb. After the baby was born, Zacharias regained his speech. The baby was John the Baptist.

Archbishop Carrillo, here to celebrate Alfonso's birthday and my name day, said Mass this morning, his booming voice filling the tiny chapel. (I tried to imagine the Archbishop struck dumb and could not.) He reminded us that soon after Gabriel told the Blessed Virgin that she had conceived a son to be named Jesus, Mary went to tell her good news to her cousin Isabel.

And Isabel said, "Blessed art thou among women, and blessed is the fruit of thy womb." Every day when I pray the rosary, I repeat the words that Isabel spoke to Mary.

After Mass, we feasted on roast venison, and there was more dancing and singing, and I felt very well satisfied with it all.

Arévalo — 16th of November 1467

Archbishop Carrillo told me this morning that troubles are brewing once again. Some of the rebels who once declared their allegiance to Alfonso have begun drifting back to Enrique's side. Among them is the Archbishop's nephew Pacheco. I can never remember whose side El Zorro is on.

"The *grandes* are tired of the conflict," the Archbishop claimed, "tired of the crime and highway robbery that make it necessary to travel with a full company of soldiers for protection. They want peace."

Which is what they wanted when Enrique tried to

marry me off to the hideous Girón. I hope no one is plotting another such scheme for me!

Arévalo — 20th of November 1467

El Zorro! Will his plots never end?

Beatríz burst into my chambers today, breathless with news: Pacheco has announced his intent to betroth one of his own daughters (he has six or seven) to the Prince of Aragón (whose name I have sworn not to mention).

I laid aside the christening gown that I am embroidering with tiny pearls and managed to prick my finger with the needle.

"And King Juan of Aragón?" I demanded. A tiny drop of blood appeared at the tip of my finger. "Is he agreeable to the betrothal?"

"He is not opposed to it. Pacheco is a very rich and powerful man. He has persuaded Enrique to give him all sorts of land and titles, including some that rightfully belong to Alfonso. Pacheco has huge armies at his command, and that is what King Juan desires."

My spirits plummeted. I know little about The Prince I

Cannot Name, but he did sound so much better than El Escorpión!

Arévalo — 19th of December 1467

Weeks pass with no further word on the subject of Pacheco's daughter and that Prince.

I see Beatríz nearly every day. But her thoughts are with the child she carries.

Arévalo — 24th of December 1467
Christmas Eve

For the Feast of the Nativity, my mother has agreed to allow us to dress her in her finest silk gown and to put up her hair in a silver net. For months she has refused to leave her chamber, and Clara and I consider it a triumph that she will accompany us to Mass and to the banquet following. Tiny oil lamps are being lighted in the windows of every home in Arévalo, from castle to humblest cottage, to welcome the Christ Child.

Alfonso is here with us. If my brother is concerned at the loss of support of the *grandes*, he does not show it. He continues to play the role of King of Castilla, but he has few subjects.

Arévalo — 6th of January 1468
The Feast of the Three Kings

We bundled up against the cold and went out to watch the parade of city officials dressed as the Wise Men from the East. They tossed sweets and coins to the children, who scrambled to collect them.

Back here we warmed ourselves and exchanged gifts. My favorite is a small chess set given to me by the Archbishop. The pieces are made of wood, marvelously carved and painted and gilded. I challenged Alfonso to a match, but he refused my challenge! I know why. He is afraid I will beat him.

But he claims it is because he must leave for Toledo.

Arévalo — 20th of January 1468

It seems that I record little but sorrow. All around is unhappiness and misery.

The country suffers from a growing hatred of the Jews.

Word is received of much bloodshed in Toledo, a day's journey south of Madrid. There, mobs have attacked and robbed any Jews and *conversos* they have encountered. Many have been killed.

Toledo is now divided into two hostile bands, the Christians against the Jews. Wise Clara, who understands so much, explained to me the cause of the resentment of the Jews and *conversos*:

"The common people denounce them for being merchants, salesmen, tailors, shoemakers, tanners, weavers, smiths, peddlers, grocers, and jewelers — in short, for making a profit without much labor. They blame the Jews for not working the soil, even though Jews are forbidden to own land. The common people do not distinguish between Jews, like Doctor Abravanel, and *conversos*, like Catalina and her family. They resent them all."

"Do you believe," I asked Clara, "that *conversos* are sincere Christians? I have heard that many continue to practice their Jewish faith in secret."

"I, too, was present when Padre Torquemada preached his sermon on that subject. You are thinking of Catalina, are you not?"

"I am," I said. "I believe with all my heart that she is a true Christian."

"As do I," said Clara. "But Catalina is but one *converso*. There are many others. She is faithful, but others may not be."

Meanwhile, the bloodshed continues in Toledo, which until now has supported Alfonso as king. Now the *alcalde*, the mayor of the town, demands a bribe for his loyalty. Alfonso is furious and refuses to bow to such demands. He has told the *grandes* of Toledo that they are free to support Enrique, if that is their wish.

I am proud of him!

Arévalo — 26th of January 1468

Catalina has begun to stitch a silk banner for Alfonso, displaying the castle and the lion of the Kingdom of Castilla and León. She has shown me the design that she has in mind. It will be quite handsome, I am sure.

I am beginning to believe that Catalina is more than half in love with my brother. This, the girl who has been insisting that she will pledge herself to a convent and devote her life to the Blessed Virgin! Alfonso seems unaware of her affection.

There has been talk in times past that my brother Alfonso is to marry Princess Juana, his own niece, but I have heard nothing more of that. Enrique, the Lion Who Changes His Mind, has probably had other thoughts of a husband for the little Princess. It would not surprise me if he intends to offer La Beltraneja to the nameless Prince of Aragón!

Arévalo — 24th of February 1468

Another Lent has begun, another forty days of prayer and fasting. Most of all I miss playing my cittern. Ana does, too.

I have not seen Padre Torquemada since I left Segovia. My confessor here, Padre Guzmán, is nearly his opposite, short and stout with a sweet smile, merry eyes, and a gentle disposition. And not at all inclined to dispense harsh penances! It would never occur to him to have me record my sins. I do not think he cares one bit about which rib God took from Adam to create Eve. "Enjoy God's love!" Padre Guzmán admonishes me with that cherub's smile. What a novel idea.

Arévalo—1st of March 1468

Outside, it rains and rains. Inside, we stitch and stitch. Beatríz suggests that I stitch more slowly, or she will have to produce twins to make use of all the little gowns I have sewed for her child.

Arévalo—12th of March 1468

The whole world is waiting. Waiting for the Resurrection of Our Lord. Waiting for the rains to stop and the green sprouts to appear in the field. Waiting for the fighting to stop between rebels and loyalists. Waiting for the birth of Beatríz's baby in a month's time.

And I — I am waiting (still!) for some word from Enrique about a betrothal for me, some bit of gossip about El Zorro and his efforts to snare the Nameless Prince for his daughter. (She must be ugly. How could she be otherwise, with such a father?)

I am waiting for something to happen. Anything!

Arévalo — 10th of April 1468
Easter Day

Alleluia, Christ is risen! He is risen indeed!

Once more the dark season of Lent has ended, the bright season of Easter begun. We celebrated with a splendid banquet, prepared and served with all pomp and ceremony.

Beatríz could not be with us. The time of the birth is at hand, and she no longer goes out in public. Don Andrés was present and received many toasts on the imminent birth of his heir.

Clara whispered to me, "Bad luck. He should pretend that nothing is happening." Instead he smiled and bowed and proposed a toast to his absent wife.

I had hoped for a new gown to wear to the banquet, but I have no money for gowns or for anything else. Alfonso made me a gift of the town of Medina del Campo, but the *alcalde* there is loyal to King Enrique and will not send the taxes and rents to me without Enrique's approval. Of course Enrique does not approve.

And so I wore last year's gown, which has grown tight around my chest and shabby as well.

Beatríz has gone into labor. We all pray for her safe delivery.

I remember well when Princess Juana was born six years ago. I was a member of the Queen's court at that time. As is the custom, the birth was attended not only by midwives and the court physician, but also by many of the *grandes* and members of the court. While the Queen squatted on the birthing stool, King Enrique stood on one side of her and Archbishop Carrillo on the other, with various other dignitaries standing by in order of rank — military men and churchmen.

Poor Queen Juana! She asked her ladies-in-waiting to place a veil over her face so that not everyone in the crowded palace room would see her grimacing. But of course that did not prevent her from crying out, and her labor was both long and hard. For once I felt pity for her.

Beatríz is not a queen and therefore can go through her labor and delivery in greater privacy. I am sure she is grateful for that! She has asked me to be with her, and I have promised that I will.

Beatríz was delivered of a sturdy baby boy sometime after midnight. She is exhausted and is sleeping now. I am tired but too excited for sleep.

The baby is to be named Rodrigo, in honor of Rodrigo Díaz de Vivar — the legendary El Cid, whom Beatríz admires as much as I do. Now baby Rodrigo has been taken away to be suckled by the wet nurse chosen by Beatríz. She interviewed at least a dozen women before making her choice.

"The child swallows character and disposition along with the breast milk," Beatríz reminded me.

"And what of intelligence?" I asked. "Does breast milk carry that as well?"

"Let me just say, Doña Isabel," Beatríz confided only a few days ago, "that if I had my way, I would suckle the child myself, to ensure that it receives everything I have to offer. That would include intelligence."

"And courage," I added, remembering Beatríz with her hidden dagger at my near-betrothal to Girón.

"Courage, too. But everyone is against my idea. Andrés was shocked when I suggested it, as was my mother. And I have not the courage to defy convention. So I have hired a woman of placid disposition and excellent character, and hope that I have chosen well."

Arévalo — 20th of April 1468

Little Rodrigo was baptized today in the royal chapel. I stood as his godmother while Archbishop Carrillo dipped the baby into the baptismal font, made the Sign of the Cross on the baby's forehead with consecrated oil, and solemnly pronounced his name. Rodrigo screeched with the fullness of his lungs — a good sign, they say.

I know that Beatríz wanted Alfonso to be one of the baby's godfathers, but Don Andrés was opposed; his choice was Enrique. Beatríz proposed — wickedly — that both be asked, since there are customarily two godfathers. But of course such a thing is not possible. My two brothers do not speak to each other.

In the end, Clara's husband, Gonzalo Chacón, and one of Andrés's brothers made the vows as godparents.

Today I am seventeen. My life hangs suspended between childhood and womanhood. The question of a husband remains without answer. In some ways I cherish my freedom, but at the same time I worry about my future.

Under the direction of Catalina, my ladies-in-waiting enacted a little play in observance of my birthday. Each took the part of one of the Seven Cardinal Virtues: Faith, Hope, Charity, Wisdom, Courage, Temperance, and Justice. (Since there are six ladies, Alicia was both Faith and Justice.) I found it very tedious and dull but of course pretended to be deeply moved.

My mother has given me a Book of Hours for my private devotions, the text for the prayers and psalms illuminated by monks in gold and brilliant colors.

Lately, the Queen Widow has seemed unusually lucid and in possession of her reason, for which I am grateful. It is at these times we can talk. But when the lightness fades from her spirit and darkness returns, I am downcast again.

Alfonso, knowing of my interest in the movements of the stars and planets across the sky, presented me with an illustrated chart of the heavens. And Catalina has worked in fine silks and gold thread a depiction of Eve in the Garden of Eden. Eve holds a golden apple, and the wily Serpent glides among the leaves of the Tree of Knowledge. He reminds me of El Zorro, Juan Pacheco.

Beatríz, not yet recovered from the birthing, sent a set of fine writing quills with a silver knife to sharpen them, all in an embroidered silk pouch. I know that she intends me to use them not only to write letters, but to write in this book, which is known only to her. I keep it hidden in my bedchamber between my mattresses, where it will be found only by the maids (including Ana) who cannot read anyway and would likely mistake it for a book of prayers.

Arévalo — 25th of April 1468

I learned today from Archbishop Carrillo that King Enrique has had several offers for my hand in marriage. One is from an Englishman — Richard, Duke of Gloucester, younger brother of King Edward. I know nothing of him or of the others.

There is always El Escorpión, who now demands that I marry him to make up for some supposed slight to his niece, little Princess Juana. (Not so little anymore. She is six years old and — the last I saw her — with a tongue as sharp as her mother's.) Imagine, marrying someone as a means of apology!

Arévalo — 1st of May 1468

Our joy at the birth of Beatríz's baby has been tempered by word of a fresh outbreak of the Black Death. A messenger brought news from Madrid that cases of the plague have been reported in towns to the south. Several have been closed.

Immediately a chill of fear swept through our small town. Every few years another outbreak of the pestilence snatches away many lives. A century before I was born, the Black Death was brought from Constantinople by the Crusaders returning from their Holy War against the Muslims. The plague carried away thousands upon thousands of people throughout Europe. Since then there has been nothing quite so terrible, for which we thank God. But at every eruption we fear the worst.

There is no cure for the illness. Even the Jewish physicians do not know how to treat it. The victim suffers from high fever and chills and quickly falls into a delirium. Then lumps appear in the armpits and the groin — they are called buboes — and the infected blood that pours from them is black. Death comes in a matter of days.

There is nothing to do but shut the town where the disease has appeared, and for forty days allow no one to enter or to leave. One can only pray for those sealed inside.

Arévalo — 6th of May 1468

Worried as we are about the Black Death, there are other worries as well! Alfonso continues to lose support among the *grandes.*

Most disappointing for my younger brother is the loss of Toledo. He speaks often now of his desire to regain it, and I have promised to do what I can to help him. Even though I left Enrique's captivity, for many months I have tried to remain neutral in the rivalry between my two brothers. But the time has come for me to declare myself on Alfonso's side. He is clearly the better ruler.

Arévalo — 15th of May 1468

The Black Death moves closer to Madrid. The gates of Ocaña have been closed, as well as those of several towns to the west.

So far the epidemic remains far to the south of us, and we are not yet too alarmed.

Arévalo — 23rd of May 1468

Every day brings notice of more deaths and the closing of more towns. We offer Masses daily for those who have died and those who suffer, and we pray that we may be spared.

My ladies-in-waiting are frightened. I try to calm them, to assure them that all will be well, that we must place our trust in God.

Arévalo — 26th of May 1468

To distract myself, I daily visit my little godson, Rodrigo, a chubby child with a happy disposition. Beatríz has chosen her wet nurse well. She is a jolly soul whose presence cheers us.

Every day I visit my mother, who sometimes speaks to me with perfect clarity and sometimes seems not to know me, her eyes as vacant and untroubled as the sky above us. On occasion she will allow me to take her outside into the fresh air, out of the gloom and mustiness of her chamber. But she complains that the sunlight hurts her eyes, or if it is night, that it is too dark to see anything, and so we always return quickly. Then she asks me to play for her upon my cittern, even though it causes her to weep.

Arévalo — 1st of June 1468

That Catalina loves Alfonso is increasingly plain. It shows in her eyes, the way they shine when my brother walks into the chapel, and they remain fastened on him until he leaves again. She has not spoken of it to me.

Alfonso is halfway between fourteen and fifteen, every day less of a boy and more of a man. He is already quite tall and may someday reach the same height as our brother Enrique. His shoulders are still narrow, but his hair is thick and blond, his features finely wrought. What girl would not fall in love with him! But of course, anything but a sweet, brief romance at a distance is out of the question. When he marries, his wife must be of royal blood. Catalina's family is not of that rank.

Arévalo — 7th of June 1468

Alfonso complains that weeks go by without his receiving any word whatever of the movements of Enrique's soldiers. El Zorro is once again on Alfonso's side! How Alfonso and Carrillo can tolerate Pacheco is beyond my understanding.

Arévalo — 24th of June 1468

In ten days Alfonso leaves for Ávila, where he hopes to recruit fresh troops. I will go with him. He has sworn to retake Toledo.

It will be just a small group of us. Catalina insists on going, too, despite her difficulties! I have done my best to persuade her to stay here, telling her that she can be of help to Beatríz and the baby. I especially need her to help Clara look after my mother.

She will not heed me. Alfonso will have to order her to stay behind.

Arévalo — 29th of June 1468

A change of plan: Alfonso and I leave in a few hours, before sunrise. The reason: an outbreak of plague here in Arévalo. Already there are rumors of several deaths, and the council will surely order the gates closed by noon.

Clara is distraught, as is Catalina, who has been ordered by my brother to stay here. I am worried about all of them, but I believe that if they remain indoors, away from the breezes that may carry the pestilence, they will be safe. Catalina particularly worries me, for she has a feverish look. It may be only lovesickness for my brother. She moons after him, and he takes no notice of her whatsoever. It would be amusing if it were not so sad.

I must finish my packing and make sure this book is not left behind, but travels with me. I have decided to leave Ana and my cittern here. She is to play for my mother in my absence.

Cardeñosa — 30th of June 1468

We are all exhausted. We have arrived safely at the home of the *alcalde* of Cardeñosa, still an hour distant from Ávila.

It was a hard ride from Arévalo to reach the village before dark. We left in such haste that there was no time this morning to hear Mass, but Archbishop Carrillo said Mass for us under the trees when we stopped to rest.

Our hosts are most generous. The *alcalde* and other prominent citizens have given us their finest accommodations and outdone themselves in their hospitality. As soon as we had a chance to refresh ourselves, a delicious dinner was served. It happened to be Alfonso's favorite dish, trout, stuffed with spices and grilled for him by the host himself. I myself was too overcome with fatigue to have more than just a few olives and some bread with a little watered wine.

Tomorrow we continue to Ávila.

Cardeñosa — 1st of July 1468

Alfonso has fallen ill. His attendants came to my chamber at daybreak, crying out that they could not awaken him. I threw on a robe and rushed to his chamber, where Carrillo and Pacheco were already at his bedside. He lay perfectly still.

"Has he a fever?" I asked, but no one seemed to know.

"A physician has been summoned," Pacheco said.

When I laid my hand on his brow, it was not hot to the touch. "Alfonso! Alfonso!" I whispered in his ear, and then I spoke louder and louder until I was crying out his name. He did not stir.

All of us fell to our knees, led in prayer by Archbishop Carrillo. Soon the chamber was crowded with supplicants.

Presently, a physician arrived and ordered us removed. I refused to leave, as did the Archbishop and Pacheco. We three watched as the physician attempted to bleed my brother, cutting veins in both arms to remove the impure blood. But no blood flowed from his veins. His breath and heartbeat continued, but he could not be roused from his stupor.

"The plague," I whispered to Carrillo. "He is dying of the plague."

"Perhaps," Carrillo muttered. "Perhaps it is something else."

But what else could it be? The doctor continued to examine Alfonso and discovered that his tongue had turned black. Strangely, though, there are no swollen buboes in his armpits and groin.

Whatever has struck down my dearest brother, we can do nothing but pray, which I do most fervently.

Cardeñosa — 2nd of July 1468

My brother barely clings to life. I have scarcely left his side. Gazing at his still features, I wonder about those we left in Arévalo — my mother, Beatríz and her family, Catalina, Ana — and I pray for them as well.

Cardeñosa — 3rd of July 1468

Word has spread throughout the Kingdom of Alfonso's mortal illness. From all over Castilla and León, we receive messages that prayers are being said night and day for his return to health. But there is no change.

Cardeñosa — 4th of July 1468

The physician says nothing can be done. It is God's will. The end is near. I try to brace myself for the worst. I cannot imagine this world without Alfonso.

Cardeñosa — 5th of July 1468

At three o'clock this afternoon, my beloved brother, Alfonso, King of Castilla and León, gave up his soul to Almighty God. May he now rest in peace.

Ávila — Convent of Santa Ana
6th of July 1468

I am stunned by this terrible thing that has happened. Within a few hours of his death, Alfonso's corpse was carried back to Arévalo, to the Convent of San Francisco, outside the walls of the town. There the nuns are preparing it for burial. Carrillo and Pacheco would not permit me to accompany my brother's body. Instead I have been moved into the Convent of Santa Ana.

"It is for your own protection, Doña Isabel," insisted Archbishop Carrillo. I assumed he meant that I would be safer there from the Black Death, but he soon corrected me. "I mean that you need protection from Enrique's *caballeros*," he said. "You understand, do you not, Doña Isabel, that you are now next in line for the throne?"

But I am too overcome by grief to understand anything but the pain of the loss of my brother.

Ávila — 8th of July 1468

The pestilence sweeps across our land, and there is no telling who shall be taken and who shall be spared. It is said that at the very hour Alfonso passed to his Glory, many others died in Arévalo and Segovia. Those departed souls, especially the children, are now in the King's company before God's throne.

Among those whose spirits are with Alfonso is my dearest friend Catalina. I felt that she was unwell when I bade her good-bye a week ago. Beatríz writes that on the same day that Alfonso was stricken, Catalina fell ill. She lingered for days, then died. Could she have known that her beloved was mortally ill? I believe she yearned to be with him in heaven as she could not be with him on earth.

I wept again at this news, remembering how her prayers had helped me escape the fate of betrothal to Girón, and how we had pledged to make a pilgrimage to Zaragoza. Now I must make that pilgrimage alone.

Beatríz assures me of the continuing health of Andrés

and Rodrigo and also of my mother, who responded to the tragic news of my brother's death with no words, only silent tears. I seem to do nothing but weep.

Ávila — 9th of July 1468

At Carrillo's insistence I have written to the *grandes* who supported Alfonso as king, reminding them that I am Alfonso's rightful heir. The Archbishop dictated my words: "That which was due my brother Alfonso is now due me." Carrillo and Pacheco added their signatures to mine, and the messengers rode off to deliver the letters. I am uncertain of this claim, but Carrillo was adamant.

Ávila — 13th of July 1468

It is a consolation for me to be lodged here in the monastery with the nuns, especially their kindly old abbess. In happier times I have stayed with them to study their fine needlework. Now I can do nothing but think and pray most fervently.

I beg God's guidance as I look to a future much altered by the death of dear Alfonso.

Ávila — 14th of July 1468

God has heard my prayers and sent me an answer, and it is this: *The death of Alfonso is a sign of God's displeasure at the rebel cause. As long as Enrique lives, no other has a right to wear the crown.*

Ávila — 15th of July 1468

I had just completed my morning prayers from the Book of Hours when the old abbess appeared at my chamber. "Doña Isabel! You have visitors! Archbishop Carrillo and his company are waiting for you below."

Dressed in a long white woolen gown that I shall wear for the first month of mourning, I followed the abbess as she hobbled down a gloomy passageway. An ornate iron gate separates the cloister from the outside world. On the other side of the gate stood the Archbishop, arrayed in robes of silk and velvet and accompanied by dozens of richly dressed knights.

I went as far as the gate. When they saw me, Carrillo and the *caballeros* dropped to their knees. "Doña Isabel," the Archbishop said somberly, "it is our most humble request that you take the rebel throne in the place of your late brother. Will you consent to become Queen Isabel of Castilla and León?"

With the strength that God gave me, I had my answer ready. First I thanked them. Then, my voice trembling, I said, "I believe that God wishes me to be Enrique's heir, not his rival. I have written to tell him this."

Archbishop Carrillo reeled backward as though I had struck him. For a moment he seemed unable to speak. Then he recovered himself. "Is it possible that you have been driven mad with grief?" he asked incredulously.

"Be assured that I have not, Your Grace," I replied. "My reason is sound."

Carrillo arose and approached the iron gate, a tall and commanding figure. He had grown quite red in the face. "For four difficult years, your brother and I and others have struggled for the rebel cause. Would you put an end to all that so easily?" His tone was steady, but I could sense the anger beneath his gentle words.

"I would put an end to the unrest," I said. "I desire nothing more than peace in the Kingdom."

The Archbishop grasped the gate. We faced each other, only inches apart. "Doña Isabel, please listen," he coaxed.

"King Juan of Aragón has sent me this message: If you consent to marry the Prince, the King will support the rebel cause."

I felt my heart being torn in two: I want to marry Fernando, but I cannot support the rebels. Behind me I could hear the clack of the abbess's wooden beads as she paced nervously.

"I have promised Enrique that I will not oppose him," I said. "I shall be Enrique's successor, not his rival."

"You shall if King Enrique does not decide to name little Princess Juana his successor in your stead, Doña Isabel," the Archbishop said curtly. "Then you might wish you had heeded my advice."

I looked at him steadily. "Forgive me, Your Grace."

The Archbishop bowed. At length he and his men mounted their horses and rode away, and I retired to my chamber and fell once more upon my knees in prayer.

Ávila — 30th of July 1468

Poor Enrique! I cannot help but pity him! Nothing ever seems to go well for him.

More than a year ago, he sent Queen Juana to live in

Coca, at the castle of Bishop Fonseca. Now she has fallen in love with Fonseca's nephew, and is said to be expecting his child! So she is in disgrace, and I have heard — all this from Carrillo — that Enrique has turned his back on her. He has formally declared that his marriage to her is not and never has been legal. The end of Queen Juana!

Ávila — 3rd of August 1468

More gossip.

"Enrique is willing to name you as his heir," says Carrillo. "With news of the Queen's dishonor, rumors are again circulating that Princess Juana is not his true daughter. The people of Castilla will never accept her as their queen. They want you, Doña Isabel."

Ávila — 5th of August 1468

I have left the convent and the simple comforts offered by the good nuns and moved to the royal castle in Ávila. The weather is so hot that I have little strength for anything. I thought to take up my sketching again, but my ladies-in-waiting let me know in small ways that they prefer to move about as little as possible. They are happiest when they are drinking strawberry water and fanning themselves. To tell the truth, so am I. Sketching only reminds me of Catalina and makes my heart ache.

Ávila — 7th of August 1468

Visits from El Zorro and El Toro. They would amuse me if they did not vex me so much.

First it was Pacheco. He was on his way to meet with Enrique to arrange a peace treaty between the rebels and those loyal to the King.

Before he departed, El Zorro leaned close to me and said softly, "I have this counsel for you, Doña Isabel: Pay no attention to any advice from Carrillo. His chief interest is in increasing his own power."

As though that were not El Zorro's chief interest, too! What a relief to see the Fox ride away.

Scarcely a day later, I had another visit from El Toro! "Be careful of Pacheco," Carrillo warned me, wagging his finger close to my nose. "He is entirely untrustworthy. You can never be sure whose side he is on."

Ávila — 13th of August 1468

For nearly a week, there have been no visits from El Toro or El Zorro or anyone else. All have gone to work out the details of the peace treaty with King Enrique. I am not consulted. My opinion is not asked for. And so I wait.

I have received several letters from Beatríz, reporting on the progress of my godson, Rodrigo. She wrote, "I look forward to the day that you, too, shall enjoy the happiness that only a child can bring. But first we must find you a brilliant <u>husband</u>!"

Immediately, I took up my pen to write a reply, but I grew so melancholy when I considered the upheaval of my life that I could think of nothing to say.

Ávila — 18th of August 1468

The treaty is drawn up, the plans made. In a month's time, I shall meet with King Enrique and his attendants to sign the documents at a place called Toros de Guisando. It is named for the four carved stone bulls that have stood guard there for many centuries. I have not seen my brother in more than a year, and I have no idea what to expect from him.

I remember when we were once close, or at least cordial to one another. But that proper warmth seems to have melted away like snow in a rain shower, and for some time there has been little but coldness between us.

Ávila—17th of September 1468

I have not slept much or eaten well in days. Tomorrow I meet with King Enrique. I shall wear a new gown, amber-colored cut velvet with a cloak of dark green damask. I will be mounted on a black mule with trappings of black velvet trimmed in silver and gold. To show honor to my rank as future queen, Archbishop Carrillo says he will walk beside me, holding the golden reins. On either side of us will ride the bishops of two cities that support me. Two hundred *caballeros* will troop behind us.

I am nervous but try to conceal it. I pray that all goes well.

Ávila—19th of September 1468

All did go well, the ceremonies are finished, and now we shall see what happens.

Compared with King Enrique, my company made a modest appearance indeed. He arrived at the open field outside the city amid trumpet fanfares with an escort that included <u>thirteen hundred</u> horsemen!

El Zorro trotted by his side, leading a group of bishops and dozens of *grandes* and lesser nobles. Among them was Andrés de Cabrera, husband of my dear Beatríz. One of the reasons that I so desire a peaceful accord with my brother is that I cannot bear to have families and friends separated by civil war.

With trembling legs I dismounted and approached Enrique and bent to kiss his hand. (Even in the midst of all this splendor, the King's clothes are as drab as ever.) But Enrique waved me away and smiled, brother to sister. He has never liked ceremony, and I was deeply touched that no ceremony separated us now.

But Carrillo! What a stubborn man he is! He refused to kiss the King's hand. Embarrassed, I whispered, "Your Grace, as a kindness to me, please honor the King."

And in a booming voice that could be heard by all, the Archbishop announced, "I shall kiss the King's hand only after he has sworn you as his one and only heir."

I was shocked. So was everyone! But Enrique seemed not to notice the insult, or if he noticed, he did not mind, or if he minded, he did not respond. We all moved to a table under a silken tent set up in the middle of the field. The documents were ready to be signed.

I promised to respect Enrique as my King, Lord, and Sovereign.

Enrique promised to cancel his promise to Queen Juana that Princess Juana would inherit the throne, and he promised to make me his heir to the Kingdom of Castilla and León.

Then Enrique promised me several towns and their rents and taxes. I am to receive even Madrid, but only after a year, to make sure that I keep my part of the bargain.

And this is the fourth promise: Enrique may not force me to marry against my will, and I have agreed not to marry without his approval.

The ceremony went on (and on and on). Enrique swore me in as Princess of Asturias (this was once Princess Juana's title) and future Queen of Castilla and León. Representatives of the clergy, the nobility, and the common people all stepped forward, bowed, and kissed my hand three times, signifying their loyalty. The Pope's envoy pronounced a blessing, trumpets blared, everyone cheered, and at last Carrillo bent to kiss Enrique's hand. And Enrique, being Enrique, smiled at the Archbishop and waved him away.

So all ended happily. I hope it lasts.

Cadalso de la Vidrios — 20th of September 1468

We are here at Enrique's camp to celebrate our reconciliation and the end of the civil war. I have not seen my brother like this in a very long time. An ox roasts on an enormous spit, and minstrels wander through the crowd. People are singing and dancing and beg me to join them, which I do. It is as if the unhappy times of the past have been forgotten.

But not everyone is pleased. Yesterday after the ceremony, Archbishop Carrillo, looking tired and dispirited, announced that he was returning to his estate at Yepes, south of Madrid. He left me with a stern warning.

"I do not believe that King Enrique will keep his word.

At the first opportunity he will cancel this treaty and again declare Princess Juana his successor."

"You are wrong," I said firmly. "My brother has sworn to it."

The Archbishop shrugged. "I know that you do not believe me, Doña Isabel. But you will see. Finally, you must understand," he continued wearily, "that it is most important now that you marry. And the sooner the better."

"Then whom should I marry, Your Grace?" I teased, knowing the answer he would give.

"Prince Fernando," he replied without hesitation.

Ocaña — 1st of October 1468

At Enrique's bidding I have moved once more, this time to Ocaña, which lies south of Madrid, across the Tajo River. I dared not object, because Enrique has brought his court here and has promised to summon the *grandes* to recognize me formally as his heir.

I had to leave my dear mother at Arévalo, and also Ana, of whom my mother has grown quite fond. Ana plays for her, and my mother sometimes mistakes Ana for <u>me</u>.

At least my old nurse-governess Clara is with me. Her

husband's nephew is Gutierre de Cárdenas, in whose handsome palace we are staying. His wife, Leonora, has become one of my ladies-in-waiting. A witty and clever woman, she reminds me of Beatríz. Cárdenas is a kind and intelligent man who bows and smiles and pretends he is loyal to Enrique. Beneath the smiles he is a rebel who wants to see my brother dethroned.

We are only half a day's journey from Archbishop Carrillo's estate at Yepes, but El Toro is distressed that I have not followed his wishes and has not called on me.

Ocaña — 9th of October 1468

This is all Pacheco's doing! He has surrounded me with spies, palace servants whom he has bribed — the guard at the palace gate, the maidservant who empties the slops, the assistant to the carver, and who knows who else.

Clara agrees. "Trust Carrillo to help you. I learned from my servants that the Archbishop has also placed spies here in my nephew's palace. The spies are spying on the spies!"

Just three weeks ago, we signed a peace treaty at Toros de Guisando, but the battles are still being fought — only secretly now, beneath the surface.

Ocaña — 25th of October 1468

Such an uproar! This morning a servant found a sign nailed to the main gate of the palace. "The Treaty of Toros de Guisando is unlawful. Princess Juana is the rightful heir of King Enrique," the notice reads. "This notice has been distributed throughout the Kingdom." I immediately sent a message to Enrique, but the King has gone hunting and left Pacheco to sort things out.

Ocaña — 30th of October 1468

Now I know who is behind the notices: Queen Juana! The tale has gone from mouth to ear so many times that it may be untrue in part. But then, with Queen Juana, anything is possible. Here it is:

When the Queen learned about the treaty, she had one of her famous temper tantrums. Although in a delicate condition with child, the Queen made a daring escape from Bishop Fonseca's castle. Only a few weeks from the expected birth, she had her servants lower her in a basket from a window. The ropes broke and the basket crashed to the ground, but the Queen escaped unharmed and fled to the home of a sympathetic nobleman. It is this *grande* and his friends who are responsible for the notice.

Sly Pacheco tells me not to worry. He has a plan but will not yet say what it is.

Ocaña — 2nd of November 1468

I am so angry I can scarcely write.

This is Pacheco's plan: Point One, I am to marry El Escorpión. Point Two, Princess Juana is to marry El Escorpión's son, Prince João of Portugal. Then, if I have a male child, my son will inherit the throne. But if I do not have a son and Princess Juana does, then <u>her</u> son will become the next king of Castilla. What El Zorro does not mention is that with me safely married to the Portuguese king, he can marry his homely daughter to Fernando.

"King Enrique has approved the plan," said Pacheco, bowing. "By his order I have written to the King of Portugal of your interest in marriage. I urged him to send his ambassadors as soon as possible to settle the matter." El Zorro showed his little fox teeth in a false smile. "I am sure that My Lady Princess will be pleased to have this important matter of her future settled once and for all."

I felt like slapping his face.

I see clearly now how right Archbishop Carrillo has been all along. His predictions have all been fulfilled.

As soon as the wretched El Zorro had left my presence, I sent an urgent message to the Archbishop, humbly begging his pardon and asking to meet with him.

Ocaña — 12th of November 1468

The kind feelings that I thought were growing between my brother and me two months ago have turned completely sour. The towns he promised have not been turned over to me. Without the rents and taxes, I have no money to set up my own household, hire servants, or do any of the things that I am entitled to as Princess of Asturias. So the title means nothing.

Now he has broken his word and intends to force me to marry El Escorpión after all. But I am determined <u>not</u> to marry him, no matter what Enrique commands.

Oh, I do so need the counsel of Carrillo! Even if he says, "I told you so."

Ocaña — 17th of November 1468

News from Leonora, who heard it from her husband, Cárdenas: Queen Juana has borne a son who is not Enrique's (her second child under such circumstances, if the rumors about La Beltraneja are true). She has also managed to infuriate everyone with her outrageous demands, including the noble gentlemen who supported her. Now no one is on her side, and El Zorro's stupid Portuguese marriage plan for Princess Juana is off.

Ocaña — 29th of November 1468

Pacheco's scheme for Princess Juana may have failed, but the ambassador and the Bishop of Lisbon have just arrived from Portugal to arrange for my betrothal to El Escorpión. At the same time, the ambassador from Aragón came to ask for my hand in marriage to Prince Fernando. It is all too much.

Carrillo, informed of this by his spies, sent me a carefully worded message, which I understand is an invitation to come for a visit. Leonora is arranging for me to travel in disguise, and I shall leave for Yepes as soon as she tells me that everything is in order. This time I shall do whatever the Archbishop advises.

Yepes — 6th of December 1468
Carrillo's Castle

A sharp wind was blowing as my party, dressed as traveling minstrels, left Ocaña early this morning for Yepes. I carried a cittern borrowed from Leonora. Soon we were enveloped in swirling snow. We were chilled to the bone, incapable of producing a single tune, when we arrived at the gates of this forbidding fortress.

The Archbishop greeted me cordially, as though there had been no discord between us, and led me to the vast chamber that is his library.

On a wall hangs a portrait of Carrillo in the splendid robes of an Archbishop, a jeweled miter on his head and an enormous gold cross in his hand. Near the portrait stands the cross itself. While I warmed myself by a brass brazier filled with glowing coals, the Archbishop sent for a flagon of hot spiced wine.

I did not wait for the wine to be brought before I began pouring out my heart. "You are right, Your Grace," I confessed. "You were right all along about Enrique and the promises he made at Toros de Guisando. He has broken all of them."

The Archbishop took my hand. "I regret to say, Doña Isabel, that I have never trusted the King — not at Toros de Guisando, and certainly not now. We must do all we can to make sure that you are the true and only heir to the throne."

I felt like weeping, but I struggled not to show what is called "feminine weakness."

"What must I do?" I asked.

"Tomorrow we will discuss this — after you have had a hearty meal and a good night's rest."

Yepes — 7th of December 1468

The storm continues to howl around us, and we cannot return to Ocaña until it abates. This morning the Archbishop invited me again to his library. I expected to discuss my betrothal to Fernando, but the Archbishop had other things on his mind. A geography lesson!

Spread out on his table was a chart. "I have been studying the world," he said, smiling. "Look here, Doña Isabel. To the east, the vastness of Asia, from which come those spices you enjoy so much! To the south, the land of the Moors and Africa, from which your suitor, the King of Portugal, brings us gold. To the west, the Ocean Sea. Beyond it, *Terra Incognita,* the Unknown Land."

"Do you believe there are lands beyond the sea?" I asked doubtfully.

"I do. I believe that God wills us to find these lands and to claim them in His name. Gold, jewels, treasures beyond imagining! And all those souls who have not yet heard the Word of God! We need only a ship or two and a few sailors brave enough to undertake the journey. And imagine this, Doña Isabel: that the world is not flat, like this chart, but round, like a ball."

From a bowl on the table, the Archbishop seized a pomegranate. Next he snatched up a quill, dipped it in an ink pot, and began to draw on the leathery skin of the fruit. I watched him curiously.

"Now, this is Castilla" — he jabbed at a spot on the pomegranate — "and this is the Ocean Sea. And <u>here</u>" — he turned the fruit over in his hand — "is another world!"

This made no sense to me. "But I have heard that the earth is flat," I said.

"Learned men no longer believe that. The earth is

round, like this pomegranate. A ship that sails to the West will eventually reach the East." He demonstrated with his quill. "If I were a younger man, Doña Isabel, I would find a way to prove this. Perhaps when you are queen, the subject will hold more interest for you."

"But I shall never be queen if we do not solve the problem of finding me a suitable husband," I countered.

"Then you must do as I advise." He placed the ink-stained pomegranate back in the bowl. "Return to Ocaña. Smile and flatter, pretend to agree, but promise nothing," he said firmly, "while I find a way for you to marry Fernando." He smiled. "Now, Doña Isabel, could I interest you in a game of chess?"

Before the storm ended, he had won the first game, I had won the second, and the third was a draw.

Ocaña — 9th of December 1468

Everything white, everything pure! Today on our journey homeward, I was so inspired by the beauty of a world transformed by snow bending tree branches and blanketing walls and turrets, that I have resolved to find my pens and ink and sketch God's glorious new creation.

Ocaña — 11th of December 1468

Last summer my ladies complained of the heat when I wished to go out sketching. Now they beg off because of the cold! All but Leonora, dear soul, who bundles herself up and seems happy to be away from the palace and out in the sparkling air.

But my sketches are wretched, miserable! I blame it on my clumsy fingers, numb with cold. Leonora admires them but does say that perhaps I should wait until spring.

Ocaña — 16th of December 1468

Last night I received a secret visit from King Juan's ambassador, Pierres de Peralta. It was a dangerous mission. He had waited on the far side of the river until he could cross under cover of darkness. But his small boat was nearly swept away by the swift current. Clara's husband, Gonzalo Chacón, and his nephew, Cárdenas, met the ambassador on the riverbank and led him to the palace. They smuggled him through the main courtyard and upstairs to my chambers. There I waited behind drawn curtains with only a single candle burning.

The ambassador, drenched and shivering, kissed my hand. Clara brought him a blanket, and we took seats around a small table and spoke in whispers.

"Esteemed Princess Isabel," said Peralta, "is it your wish to wed Fernando, Prince of Aragón and King of Sicily?"

"It is, My Lord Ambassador," I replied. "It must be Prince Fernando and no other."

"Be assured then, dear lady," Peralta said, "that I and your trusted friends" — by that he meant Carrillo, Cárdenas, and Chacón — "are doing all we can to arrange your betrothal to Fernando."

I thanked him heartily for his trouble.

"In the meantime, Doña Isabel," he said, "you must continue to behave to the ambassador from Portugal and the Bishop of Lisbon as though you are seriously considering marriage to their King."

My visitors left as silently as they had come.

Tomorrow I go on stage. Never in my life have I had to play such a role.

Ocaña — 21st of December 1468

Each morning I dress in a velvet gown, catch up my hair in a golden net, and prepare to smile sweetly at the Portuguese ambassador and his bishop. Underneath I am seething! I am ready to scream! But I have become a great player, surprising myself most of all.

All this to find a way to marry a man of whom I still know next to nothing!

Ocaña — 24th of December 1468

Leonora is busy preparing a great banquet to celebrate the birth of the Christ Child as the season of Advent draws to an end. This is our last night of fasting.

The Portuguese are still here. Leonora says they are growing impatient, tired of waiting for my reply.

"My husband tells them, 'Young women of Castilla are modest,'" Leonora says, laughing. "'They wait for the decision about marriage to be made by their elders.'"

"But that is true," I said as I accompanied her to inspect the boar being roasted for tomorrow's feast. "Did you not wait for your father's choice of your husband?"

"He thought I did. But I had already made up my mind to marry Gutierre."

She reminds me of Beatríz when she speaks like this.

Ocaña — 25th of December 1468

Archbishop Carrillo came to say Mass for the Feast of the Nativity. King Enrique joined us, and we celebrated with a banquet and singing and dancing as though nothing unusual were going on. For this one day, at least, we seemed as close as brother and sister should be. I allow myself to hope for a full reconciliation.

Ocaña — 28th of December 1468

Wrong! Wrong! Wrong! And on which spies can I blame this?

Somehow Enrique has learned of my intent to wed Fernando. He sent one of his men to threaten me with imprisonment if I do not leave the decision of a husband to him. Then he told the Portuguese ambassadors that they should simply carry me back to Lisbon with them.

Finally, Enrique swore that he would lock me up in the

castle in Madrid if I continued to defy him, but he stopped short of that because he knows Carrillo would send troops to protect me.

Ocaña — 6th of January 1469, The Feast of the Three Kings

The Portuguese ambassadors finally gave up and went home — without me.

I fret day and night, worrying about my decision to defy King Enrique.

Worse, I remember that last year, my brother Alfonso was with us in Arévalo for the feast day. He gave me a rosary with beads of ivory, which I use every day. Now he is gone, and my life has changed more than I could have imagined.

Ocaña — 13th of February 1469

The betrothal papers have been signed. I am to marry Fernando. Everything is official but still secret.

Before he left my chambers to make his way back to

Carrillo's castle, the ambassador from Aragón requested that I write a letter to Prince Fernando. He will carry it back to Zaragoza with him. Mindful that the letter might be seized by spies, I took care to word most carefully this first letter to my intended husband:

"To My Lord, King of Sicily," I wrote, "Since the ambassador is traveling to you, it is not necessary for me to write more, except to apologize for such a delayed answer. You will understand the reason from him." I hesitated for a moment before I added the last line, "From the hand that will do as you may order," and signed it, "The Princess."

Ambassador Peralta slipped the letter into the folds of his cloak, took his leave, and stepped out into the black night. Tomorrow he returns to Aragón.

Now I can do nothing but wait.

Ocaña — 6th of March 1469

Still I wait. No word yet from Aragón.

I am stitching a little holy picture to celebrate the anniversary of the baptism of my godson, Rodrigo, who will be one year old in a few weeks. Beatríz writes that he is healthy and happy and taking his first steps. I do so yearn for the time when I shall be able to write such joyous news of my own!

Ocaña — 8th of April 1469

In two weeks I shall be eighteen. Time moves exceedingly slowly. I am so tired of having my every action spied upon and reported to El Zorro, who then passes it on to Enrique.

Ocaña — 22nd of April 1469

Beatríz paid me a birthday visit. Little Rodrigo toddled by his mother's side. When he caught sight of me, he smiled and reached up his chubby arms to me. He is impossible to resist.

At first I hesitated to tell my dear friend of my marriage plans, because her husband is one of Enrique's closest associates. In the end I trusted that her loyalty to me would seal her lips.

"Do you still write in your book?" she asked me, and I told her I do.

"Then please copy this message onto its pages," she said, and gave me this note:

> *My dear Doña Isabel,*
>   *On the occasion of your eighteenth birthday,*
> *it is my deepest wish that your days be filled*
> *with happy events in your new life as wife*
> *and future queen.*
>
>   *Your loving friend and faithful servant,*
>   *Beatríz de Bobadilla y Cabrera*

Ocaña — 2nd of May 1469

At last! A message from King Juan — smuggled to me from Ambassador Peralta, through Carrillo, by way of Chacón. These men hold my future in their hands, while King Enrique, El León, roars outside my door.

The marriage contract is being drawn up. Carrillo has demanded a huge marriage gift for me. "It is because Castilla is so much larger and richer than Aragón,"

Chacón explains. "In a union between the two kingdoms, the future Queen of Castilla holds the advantage."

He says King Juan has agreed to the demand. I am to receive 40,000 gold florins as a betrothal gift, as well as rents and taxes from a number of wealthy towns in Aragón and Sicily, and another 100,000 gold florins after the marriage takes place.

And Prince Fernando is sending me a gold and ruby necklace that once belonged to his mother.

"And I?" I asked Clara. "What must I give in exchange?"

Clara laughed. "Yourself, Doña Isabel!" she said with delight. "Only the gift of yourself!"

"No small gift," corrected Chacón. He is a serious man, and I knew he was thinking of my position as future queen. "The question is, <u>when</u> will you receive the marriage gift? King Juan refuses to send it until you are free of Enrique's control. Until you are, you might suddenly find yourself married off to the Portuguese. Or to the French."

"The French?" This took me completely by surprise. "What about the French?"

Chacón glanced at his wife, who shook her head, and then back at me. "You have still another suitor. Charles,

Duke of Berry, brother of King Louis XI, wants to marry you. The French ambassador arrived two days ago to meet with Enrique."

So I must do more play-acting. I wonder when I shall receive the ruby necklace?

Ocaña — 5th of May 1469

King Enrique sent for me this morning. Fearing that I was being summoned to discuss the proposal from the Duke of Berry, I was naturally very uneasy. I have not seen my brother since Christmas, when he behaved most cordially. But only three days later, he threatened me with imprisonment!

He was seated at a table paring his nails with a little silver knife when I presented myself. Keeping my eye on the knife, I bowed to kiss his hand. As usual, he waved away the gesture. But he was not smiling.

"Doña Isabel," he began wearily, "in two days I must take my troops to Andalucía. A rebellion is brewing in the South. I shall be gone for at least a month, perhaps more. Swear to me now that you will not leave Ocaña and that you will not — <u>not</u>! — make any betrothal plans in my absence. When I return, I will arrange a suitable marriage for you. Do you so swear?"

Enrique was watching me closely, waiting for my reply. I thought for a moment: I had <u>already</u> made my betrothal plans, therefore I would not be <u>making</u> any. A small difference, but I would not be swearing a false oath.

"I do pledge my solemn word, My Lord," I said.

"Good," he said, and resumed paring his nails.

I was dismissed. Nothing said about the French suitor.

Ocaña — 9th of May 1469

Two days ago, I watched Enrique and his troops ride south in the direction of Córdoba. Today the ambassador from France presented himself formally with the proposal from the Duke of Berry. His cheeks were powdered and rouged, and I could smell his awful perfume before he even entered my chambers. I really do not like the habits of the French.

I greeted him with my false smile. I assured him that I was flattered by the Duke's offer of marriage. I promised to consider it.

"I wait for God to show me His will," I said. Then I

sighed and lowered my eyes. "But as you know, *Monsieur* Ambassador," I explained, "I can do nothing at all without the counsel of the *grandes* and the consent of my brother the King, who is away."

And what could the Frenchman reply to that? Nothing at all. I am becoming very clever at saying <u>maybe</u> in a way that could be taken for <u>yes</u> when I really mean <u>no</u>.

Ocaña — 24th of May 1469

As soon as the ambassador from France had left, I sent an urgent message to Carrillo, begging him to come see me. I knew that no one would dare turn away the Archbishop — especially when he arrived at the palace dressed as a knight and accompanied by some two hundred soldiers, as he did today.

The weather being fine, we met outdoors among the fruit trees. "Only the birds can hear," said the Archbishop, his sword clanking as we walked.

I told him of the oaths that Enrique squeezed out of me before he left, and of the visit from the French ambassador, and of what I had promised each.

"Ah, yes, the Duke of Berry," rumbled Carrillo. "I have

already sent one of my chaplains to investigate the brother of the French king."

"And? What do you know of him? Please tell me!"

"The chaplain reports that the duke is soft and pale with spindly legs and watery eyes. He is so weak and blind that he needs someone to support him. He is the opposite of Fernando in every imaginable way."

"How much longer must I bear this?" I cried. "I want so much to leave Ocaña and to make my marriage plans, and I have sworn I will not!"

"Patience, Doña Isabel," counseled the Archbishop. "We must arrange your flight from Ocaña with utmost care. I insist that we have at least part of your betrothal gift from King Juan before you make that bold move. King Juan, for his part, refuses to send a single florin until you are free of Enrique. Therefore, I beg you to be patient while I coax him."

"I will try, Your Grace," I promised. "But <u>when</u>?"

"If you leave here, Pacheco will order soldiers to seize you. As a practical matter, Doña Isabel, we need money to hire soldiers to defend you. And to persuade some powerful people to support you."

"You mean, to bribe them?"

"Indeed."

I know that he is right, and that I must listen to him. Ignoring his advice in the past has been a mistake. But I do not think I can bear to remain here another month, another day, another <u>hour</u> surrounded by spies and those who wish me ill.

Ocaña — 2nd of June 1469

It was Clara's idea. Clever Clara!

We were docilely sewing shirts to be given to the poor when Clara peered over her needlework and murmured, "On the anniversary of your brother's death on the fifth of July, do you not intend to accompany his remains from the convent at Arévalo to his final burial place in Ávila?"

"But I have given my word not to leave, Clara," I whispered, and glanced around hastily to see who might be listening. Miraculously, no one was present — or at least visible!

"Surely the King would not forbid such an errand, to honor his own brother?" she whispered back.

"You are right, Clara. It is my duty."

And thus she has set me to thinking — and plotting.

Ocaña — 8th of June 1469

What I am about to do is treason, or King Enrique will see it as treason. Last September at Toros de Guisando I pledged him my obedience. Only a month ago I promised not to leave Ocaña. Now I am ready to break both of these oaths. My reason is simple: I do not trust him, and I will no longer pretend that I do.

The plan is this: Cárdenas will bring me word when all is ready. We will travel at night by horseback, in disguise. The Archbishop has asked his friend the Bishop of Burgos and a small group of loyal *grandes* to accompany me.

Chacón will lead the party. Clara begs to go along, but her husband forbids it. I am grateful for her loyalty, but I fear that she will not be able to withstand the hardships of the long and dangerous journey. Besides, I need her to stay here.

Ocaña — 13th of June 1469

"Midnight," whispered Cárdenas at dinner. I am ready. Also a little nervous.

Madrigal — 18th of June 1469

Thank God, thank God, I am safe! Never have I been so frightened.

To recount: We left Ocaña shortly after midnight, disguised in the rough habits of monks. Clara promised to conceal my absence as long as possible. She will follow in a few days, bringing my gowns and other possessions. (In my saddle pouch I carried only this book and the gold crucifix given to me by my mother.)

The clear moonlight allowed us to travel quickly, although it also revealed us to any curious onlookers. We skirted Madrid on the southwest and stopped to rest only for a few hours at monasteries that Carrillo arranged for us along the way.

At the end of the third day, we encountered a troop of soldiers. I took care to keep my hair hidden under the monk's hood. While we refreshed our mounts, the soldiers told the Bishop that Enrique's *caballeros* had only hours earlier seized the town of Arévalo.

"Then we cannot go there," said the Bishop when the soldiers had moved on. The others agreed.

"The Queen Widow," I said. "I must find out where my Lady Mother is before we make other plans." And in spite of my aching bones, I remounted and urged my companions onward.

We spurred our horses relentlessly. Toward daybreak we stopped at a church not far from Arévalo, whose towers we could see in the distance. The old friar invited us to rest and share his simple meal of bread and cheese. Never has a feast tasted better!

In his wheezy old voice, the friar recounted the turmoil that had taken place. "The Queen Widow has gone to Madrigal," he said. He looked directly at me, although I had not identified myself. "Her attendants brought her here on the way." He shook his head sadly. "Poor thing, poor thing," he muttered, tapping his head, and I knew he was referring to my mother's madness.

Despite our weariness we rode on to Madrigal. Last night we entered the high stone gates of this town where I was born.

Madrigal — 20th of June 1469

I am staying in the castle where my mother gave birth to me. She is here with me.

Oddly, some of her memory has returned — perhaps because she has come back to a place where she once knew happiness. When we were reunited yesterday, she recognized me. That gives me great joy, although she has changed so much, aged so greatly, that I scarcely recognized <u>her</u>. Ana, my maid, was with her, for which I am grateful.

I was happy, too, to find Beatríz and Rodrigo here, safe and sound as well. After we had embraced, I remarked, "What a pleasure to be able to talk freely without spies lurking in every corner! In Segovia and then in Ocaña, I was Enrique's prisoner, and I have vowed that I never shall be again."

Beatríz, still her same outspoken self, said, "You are not yet Fernando's wife. There may be more attempts to stop this marriage. Perhaps it is time that you employ some spies of your own."

"Have you someone in mind?" I asked.

"Of course," she said, her eyes dancing with the old fire.

I know what she is thinking, but I do not yet know how to answer her.

Ávila — 30th of June 1469

Once I had rested and recovered my strength, my mother and I moved here to Ávila, where Alfonso's coffin has been taken to the cathedral.

Clara joined us today, tearfully relieved to find us all safe, as we were to see her. She reports that when word of my flight became known at Ocaña, El Zorro stormed around shouting, "You see! Now Doña Isabel has shown her hand and revealed her true intentions! She has committed treason against the Crown!"

"He immediately dispatched a messenger to Enrique," Clara continued, "asking that he be allowed to send troops to arrest you."

I could feel the blood drain from my face. "I have heard nothing," I said. "Do you know my brother's reply?"

"'Let her go for now.' That was all Enrique said: 'Let her go for now.' That made Pacheco angry, but he had to obey."

"'For now,'" I repeated. "That means trouble later."

"And <u>that</u>," said Beatríz, who was listening, "is why you must have spies, Doña Isabel."

"Yes, Isabel, you must," echoed my mother, astonishing us all.

Ávila — 5th of July 1469

To the slow beat of drums and the mournful tolling of the bells, the coffin of Alfonso, King of Castilla, was laid in his tomb. My mother, dressed in mourning garments, uttered a deep sigh that seemed to come from her very soul. She sank senseless to the stone floor of the cathedral. Only Ana's swift action saved her from injury.

Although we quickly revived her, the flashes of reason that I witnessed during the past few days have disappeared. My mother no longer remembers who I am.

Madrigal — 24th of July 1469

Hoping that the town of my birth would provide me a safe place to wait for further word from Fernando and King Juan, I returned here with my mother. I hoped, too, that this place would help heal her broken mind and spirit. Neither has proved true.

Who should arrive only days after I had managed to unpack my belongings but the French ambassador. Enrique sent him! And while I was busy repeating my empty phrases and bestowing my false smiles on *Monsieur* Ambassador, I learned that Enrique has ordered the town council to keep me here by force.

Meanwhile, Beatríz and Clara, now in my employ as "spies," announced loudly to all who could hear that they oppose my match with the Prince of Aragón and no longer wish to be in my service. With a great show of displeasure, they took themselves off to Coca and the castle of Bishop Fonseca. Fonseca's castle must be alive with intrigue — that is where Queen Juana found love a year ago.

Madrigal — 29th of July 1469

Fonseca is preparing to march his *caballeros* here to seize me. He was ordered by El Zorro.

This warning was delivered to me today by Beatríz and Clara, already back from Coca. They rushed into my chambers, flushed with excitement.

"Enough spying," Clara gasped, collapsing onto a bench. She sent a message to Cárdenas, who will go to Archbishop Carrillo for help.

"I think she was enjoying it," Beatríz confided, "until she realized the danger." Danger has never bothered Beatríz.

Now I must wait for news of my liberation or further imprisonment. And the perfumed Frenchman will not go away! What a terrible week.

Madrigal — 2nd of August 1469

As I write this, I am wearing a most magnificent necklace made of gold, set with a ruby as big as a hen's egg and red as blood, surrounded by gems and pearls. The ruby necklace belonged to Prince Fernando's mother and the queens of Aragón before her. It arrived before dawn, brought by a messenger disguised as a beggar. He also delivered to me eight thousand gold florins. The "beggar" informed me that Archbishop Carrillo is on his way with six hundred *caballeros* to rescue me.

I pray that he arrives before Bishop Fonseca.

Valladolid —9th of August 1469

I was watching from a window in the turret as Archbishop Carrillo in his scarlet cloak led his army through the town gates. Cárdenas was with him. In the distance I could see clouds of dust raised by Bishop Fonseca and his approaching soldiers. I fell on my knees and thanked God for my deliverance. Then I hurried to bid farewell to my mother, who gazed at me with empty eyes.

"Sing to her, Ana," I begged, and as I left I heard the plaintive notes of my cittern and my maid's sweet voice. Wearing the ruby necklace, I mounted a waiting horse and rode off with the Archbishop to the sound of kettle-drums and trumpets.

Our first destination was Fontiveros, not far from Arévalo. We were met at the gates by the *alcalde* and his council. "We cannot allow you to enter," said the mayor, and the councilmen nodded nervously. "We fear the King's anger if we do."

And so we rode on to Ávila, where we knew we would be welcomed.

But alas! The pestilence has once again broken out, and

in the weeks since I left Ávila, it has grown much worse. "If the town is closed, we may be trapped there," Carrillo said.

"Where then?" I asked wearily, close to tears.

"Valladolid," he said. "To the palace of Juan de Vivero. He is married to my brother's daughter, María de Acuña. We are sure of a haven there."

"The distance is far," I complained. We would have to retrace our steps through choking dust all the way past Arévalo and on through Medina del Campo.

"We have no choice, Doña Isabel."

And so to Valladolid we came, having ridden a night and a day. We arrived half an hour after the sunset, welcomed with jubilant cheers by a crowd of *grandes* and ordinary citizens.

I think that I shall never climb on a horse again.

Valladolid — 8th of September 1469

I have fully recovered, and so has Beatríz, but Clara still walks stiffly. She does not complain, though — all she talks of now is my wedding.

For several days I have been trying to compose a letter to Enrique. I have torn up a dozen sheets of parchment before managing to say what I want to say.

"Very high Prince and most powerful King and Lord," I began. To make him understand why I took the actions I did, I have gone over the events of the past year. I reminded him of the promises we made at Toros de Guisando. I want him to approve of my marriage to Fernando, and I did my best to assure him that our union will add to the glory of his realm.

On and on I wrote, page after page. Finally, an hour ago, I put my seal on the letter and sent it off with a messenger to the King in Córdoba.

Valladolid — 9th of September 1469

With great secrecy in the small hours of the morning under a full moon, Cárdenas and Chacón set off today for Aragón. They have orders from Carrillo to bring Fernando to Castilla before Enrique and Pacheco return from Córdoba.

Valladolid — 19th of September 1469

Bad news from Cárdenas. All the castles along the border that separates Aragón from Castilla and Fernando from me are in the hands of men who support Enrique.

Beatríz, Clara, and Carrillo's niece, María de Acuña, conspire to distract me from my despair. They talk of nothing but the wedding — <u>my</u> wedding. We walk in the garden — the weather is beautiful now — and my friends discuss my wedding gown. Clara thinks it should be of damask, but Beatríz argues for plain silk embroidered with jewels. María wonders how many venisons should be roasted, and how many barrels of wine to order.

All I care about is the safe arrival of my bridegroom!

Valladolid — 1st of October 1469

The moves in this chess match are played very slowly. I imagine that by now, my intended husband is on his way to me. And I imagine that by now, my furious brother may also be on his way.

Meanwhile, Beatríz and Clara have organized my ladies-in-waiting, assisted by seamstresses hired by María, to sew a new wardrobe for me. More than a dozen needles fly from first light until the candles are extinguished at midnight. I stitch with them — it makes the time go faster. All are sworn to secrecy, but I am certain that as soon as I leave the chamber, the tongues fly as fast as the needles.

Valladolid — 11th of October 1469

What relief! What joy!

Chacón and Cárdenas arrived sometime after midnight, weary but triumphant. I was awakened to greet the travelers. This is the story they told:

Five nights ago Fernando disguised himself as a mule driver and set out with five friends and a guide. No one, none of our enemies, paid him the least attention in his ragged clothes. Along the way they spotted a good omen: a pair of soaring eagles.

The journey was long but uneventful — until the group was well within the borders of Castilla. "And then," Chacón said, "three nights ago, a frightening thing happened."

Chacón and Cárdenas, traveling in advance of Fernando and his party, stopped for the night at the castle of the

Count of Trevino. Not expecting the Prince to arrive until the next day, the two travelers went to sleep. No one had warned the guard to expect more guests. When the Prince and his ragged friends approached the castle, the sentinel raised the alarm and a guard on the parapet hurled down a rock, barely missing Fernando. The noise awoke Chacón, who shouted to the guard and awoke the Count.

"What a night!" said Cárdenas, taking up the story. "Roused from his bed, the Count rushed to greet the Prince of Aragón with wax torches and trumpeters. The trumpeters made so much noise that nobody got any sleep."

"Where is the Prince now?" I asked, weak with relief.

"In the village of Dueñas, a short day's journey from here. Archbishop Carrillo is with him. He will come to you tomorrow."

Valladolid — 12th of October 1469

He is here, but I have not yet seen him. I have, though, signed several papers at the request of Carrillo, in which both the Prince and I promise to honor the Archbishop and to govern with his counsel. I do it as a daughter honors her father, for the Archbishop has indeed been a father to me.

As for my brother, I have as yet no word from him. And so while I wait to meet my prince and future husband face-to-face, I have written once more to King Enrique, begging him to approve my marriage.

But when shall I see Fernando? I am too agitated to eat.

Valladolid — 14th of October 1469

It is he! Oh, it is he! And all that I could wish!

I write this at three o'clock in the morning. My future husband has just left here to return to the castle at Dueñas, where he will stay until our wedding day.

He came here at midnight with three of his friends and entered the palace by the postern gate. Dressed in a new gown of lavender silk, stitched by my ladies under Clara's direction, and wearing the ruby necklace, I waited for him in an inner chamber, lighted by dozens of candles.

I shall never forget the moment he entered the room, led by Archbishop Carrillo. Cárdenas, hovering anxiously by my side, burst out, "That is he!"

For a moment we gazed at each other. I saw a gallant

young man of medium height with straight brown hair, intelligent eyes, a kind mouth. I liked him at once. I believe with all my heart that I shall love him.

For two hours we talked. I like his way of thinking and of speaking. He has humor, he has authority, he has imagination! I did not need two hours to know that I have made the right decision, for myself and for my kingdom. I believe that if the Archbishop had not been present, we might have rushed imprudently into each other's arms.

After our promises to marry were noted by an official, Prince Fernando took his leave — and took my heart with him. He will return in four days. Meanwhile, the whole palace buzzes like a beehive as María de Acuña oversees the preparations for my wedding.

Valladolid —18th of October 1469
The Feast of San Lucas

Fernando, Prince of Aragón and King of Sicily, rode into the city today, brilliantly dressed and escorted by thirty richly attired *caballeros*. Crowds of well-wishers had gathered to cheer him, and the sound warmed my heart.

Juan de Vivero and María have spent the past four days

preparing for this event, filling the great hall of the castle with sweet-smelling leaves and flowers and hundreds of candles. As dusk began to fall, Archbishop Carrillo read out the marriage agreement signed by Prince Fernando and King Juan. There followed a great feast for our friends, and after the feasting ended, my dear Prince returned to Dueñas to spend the night.

Tomorrow is our wedding day. We expect more than two thousand people to be with us, in addition to the *grandes* and churchmen who have helped and supported us, and the many friends who have encouraged us during these long, difficult months. I cannot even begin to name them all, but I must mention above all Clara and Beatríz (whose glowing face tells me that she is again with child).

Best of all, my mother is here, accompanied by Ana. She smiles at me and allows me to embrace her, but her eyes are vacant. I must believe that her heart understands all, even if her mind does not.

After we have exchanged wedding vows, the Archbishop will say Mass and give the nuptial blessings. From that solemn moment on, the day will be filled with festivities of every kind, a banquet to be shared by all, singing and dancing far into the night. Then my husband and I, his wife, shall retire to our bridal chamber.

Just now, as I was writing this, Beatríz came to me and said, "So, Doña Isabel, once you are become a wife, will you continue to put down your thoughts in your book?"

I had not considered this before, but I have made a decision. My life is about to change completely, and therefore I believe it is time to put aside this book. But I shall not write "The End." Instead I write —

THE BEGINNING

Epilogue

For six days and nights, while the wedding guests celebrated, Princess Isabel and Prince Fernando fell ever more deeply in love. The bride and groom were so happy they could almost forget that they had very little money — so little they had to borrow some of their wedding finery. For a while they could also forget that they had not received King Enrique's permission to marry.

When Enrique learned that Isabel had married without his consent, he was furious. One by one the King took away the towns that were Isabel's only source of income. But Fernando and Isabel remained determined that one day they would rule their kingdoms.

The first years of marriage were difficult for Isabel and Fernando. Besides being short of money, Fernando was often away for long periods, fighting battles for his father or tending to other duties in the Kingdom of Aragón.

When their first child was born on October 2, 1470, they named her Isabel. Politically, though, a daughter was not worth much. The only person who was probably pleased at the birth of a girl was King Enrique. He again decided to name Princess Juana as his heir. Later he changed his mind — one more time.

Then suddenly, King Enrique became severely ill and died a few minutes before midnight on December 11, 1474. Those with him in his last hours begged him to name his heir, but he remained silent.

When Isabel heard the news, she grieved for her brother. But her old counselor Carrillo convinced her there was not a moment to spare if she was to lay claim to the throne — not even time to summon Fernando, who was in Zaragoza. Two days after the King's death, in a ceremony in Segovia's Plaza Mayor, Archbishop Carrillo placed the jeweled crown of Castilla and León upon Isabel's head. The new Queen was wearing the ruby necklace Fernando had given her.

When Fernando returned from Zaragoza and discovered that Isabel had been crowned Queen in his absence, he was not happy to find himself "king consort" with his wife in charge. In time, though, the couple forged a true partnership that served them and their subjects well.

There was another relationship that Isabel had to work out. The hot-tempered Archbishop Carrillo did not know how to deal with the once-obedient princess who had become a strong-willed queen. In 1475, feeling that he had not been properly rewarded for all his help to the young couple, he switched his allegiance to King Afonso of Portugal. Afonso, whom Isabel had repeatedly rejected, was now betrothed to his thirteen-year-old niece, Princess Juana, "La Beltraneja." King Afonso declared war on Castilla, to protect the rights of his niece. The Portuguese king was defeated, and Archbishop Carrillo begged for and received Isabel's forgiveness.

There was no reconciliation with Princess Juana, who called herself "Princess of Castilla." Queen Isabel ordered her to stop using that title and sent the unhappy young woman to a convent. Juana always believed Queen Isabel had cheated her out of her rightful inheritance of the throne. Until the day she died, Juana signed her letters, *"Yo la Reina"* — "I the Queen."

In 1478, the King and Queen rejoiced at the birth of a

longed-for son. They named him Juan. He was followed a year later by a second daughter, whom they named Juana. A third daughter, María, was born in 1482, and the Queen's last child, Catalina, was born in 1485.

But tragedy seemed to follow Isabel's children. Her daughter, Isabel, died in childbirth; the princess's son died before his second birthday. Juan died at age nineteen. Juana succumbed to madness. Catalina, remembered as Catherine of Aragón, was the first of King Henry VIII's six wives. Only María seemed to live a happy life.

Although Queen Isabel and King Fernando accomplished much during their long reign, they are remembered best for their support of a daring Italian mariner, Christopher Columbus.

Queen Isabel died on November 26, 1504, at the age of fifty-three. At her request her body was wrapped in a Franciscan robe, which she believed would guarantee her entry into heaven. Today her remains lie in a starkly simple tomb in the Royal Chapel in Granada. At her side lies Fernando, who died in 1516.

Historical Notes

In spite of their personal tragedies, King Fernando and Queen Isabel succeeded in bringing order to their kingdoms, which had been torn apart by warring groups for many years. Although it was not officially known as Spain until much later, Fernando and Isabel had begun to think of their country as *España*.

Their primary goal was to drive out the Moors, who had first arrived in Andalucía in A.D. 711, under the leadership of Tarik ibn Zizad (Tarik the One-Eyed), a Berber general and governor of North Africa. The Moors had established communities throughout the Iberian peninsula, but they were mostly concentrated along the southern coasts. They brought with them knowledge of astronomy, agriculture, and medicine as well as new ideas of art and architecture that blended with and enriched Iberian culture.

But the Moors (Arabs, Berbers, and other North Africans) were Muslim, followers of Islam, and for eight centuries Christian rulers vowed to rid the peninsula of "unbelievers"— the Muslims and the Jews. For eight centuries every ruler had spent the wealth of his kingdom in the struggle to regain territory lost to the Moors.

Isabel and Fernando swore to succeed where every other monarch had failed. In 1481, they resumed the *Reconquista*, the Reconquest. Isabel planned the campaigns, and Fernando led the troops. Isabel had to pawn her jewelry — even the precious ruby necklace — to help pay for the Holy War. One by one they took back from the Moors every hill and valley, every town and city except the one they wanted most — Granada. Finally, in January of 1492, they triumphed. Granada was theirs, the Holy War was won, and the *Reconquista* was complete.

The year 1492 was notable for other reasons. Six years earlier an Italian navigator named Cristoforo Colombo — Cristóbal Colón in Spanish — had come to Fernando and Isabel with an idea: He proposed a new route to the Orient, "to reach the East by sailing West." But in 1486, the monarchs were caught up in the Holy War, and the man we call Christopher Columbus had to wait four months just for a chance to meet them.

When at last Columbus was presented to the King and Queen, he carried with him a map of the world he had drawn himself and a plan called "Enterprise of the Indies." At that time most educated people believed the world was round. Isabel and Fernando probably had spherical globes in their libraries. Indeed, other navigators had had the same idea — of reaching the spice-rich Indies by sailing West.

But Columbus was not like the others. Thirty-five years old, the same age as Isabel, he was as charming as he was ambitious. He convinced the monarchs that it was God's divine will that inspired him. The King and Queen realized that this was a chance to bring more heathens into the faith. The pagans of the Indies could be converted to Christianity. Fernando and Isabel agreed to consider his proposal.

For six frustrating years, Columbus waited while Isabel consulted with her advisers. These learned men were willing to believe that the ambitious mariner might reach the East by sailing West, but how could he sail back again?

Other advisers thought that humans could exist only in certain of the earth's zones and argued that all of those places had already been discovered. There was also the matter of money. Deeply involved in the *Reconquista,* the monarchs had no money to spare.

Finally, just when Columbus was about to give up and take his ideas to the French or the English, Isabel summoned him back to court. She promised him all he had asked for, including a title and a share of the profits.

On August 3, 1492, Columbus set sail with three tiny ships. On October 12, he sighted land — not an outer island of the Orient, as he thought, but San Salvador in the Bahamas. Five months later, Columbus returned to Castilla to bring the news of his discovery to the King and Queen. They greeted him with celebrations and awarded him gifts and special privileges and a new title: "Admiral of the Ocean Sea."

In October of 1493, Admiral Columbus set out on a second voyage, this time with seventeen ships and fifteen hundred colonists. He established a settlement on the island of Hispaniola (now the divided island of Haiti and the Dominican Republic), but still did not find the riches he had promised the King and Queen. His third voyage was even less successful, and he was so criticized for his poor management of the colony on Hispaniola that he was taken prisoner and hauled back to Madrid in chains. Queen Isabel ordered him released, but Columbus's reputation was badly damaged.

Finally, he embarked on a fourth voyage, betting all he had this time on sailing beyond the islands to reach the mainland of the Orient. Instead he landed on Honduras, where he and his crew suffered terrible hardships. He was finally rescued and crossed the Ocean Sea for the last time. Sick, penniless, and downhearted, Columbus died in 1506.

Called "Mother of the Americas," Queen Isabel is remembered as a visionary who changed the course of history through the voyages of Cristóbal Colón. But there was a dark side to her reign as well.

Known as *"Los Reyes Católicos"* (The Catholic Monarchs), Fernando and Isabel were devout Christians. Their religious fervor inspired them to send Columbus off to explore foreign lands, in hope of converting pagan souls to Christianity. Their fervor obliged them to expel the Muslims, even though the Moors contributed a great deal to the culture and the economy of the kingdom. This same intense piety compelled them to persecute the Jews.

Isabel believed that anyone who did not fully accept the Christian faith was guilty of the sin of heresy. She was convinced that many *conversos,* Jewish converts to Christianity, were false Christians who only pretended to believe. Isabel was determined to purify the Church and drive out the false Christians, or heretics. To do this, she established the Inquisition with the power to arrest, accuse, judge, and punish those accused of heresy. She named her childhood confessor, Tomás de Torquemada, the Inquisitor General.

Thus began one of the most terrible periods in human history. Anyone suspected by anyone else of being a heretic could be arrested. The accused had no way of knowing who their accusers were, and they were guilty until proven innocent. Many people were tortured until they confessed. The trial for heresy was called an *auto da fé* — an act of faith — a ceremony in which those believed guilty were publicly accused. Then inquisitors pronounced the sentence. The punishment was death.

Thousands upon thousands of *conversos* died during this awful time of wretched persecutions. But Fernando and Isabel were not satisfied. On March 31, 1492, about the time Columbus was preparing for his first voyage, the King and Queen signed an edict giving all Jews just four months to be baptized. Those who refused were forced to leave Castilla and Aragón. Some agreed to be baptized, but most fled. This is known as a *diaspora*, from a Greek word meaning dispersion or scattering. France and England refused to allow the expelled Jews to enter their countries. Many Jews went to Portugal (but when forced to convert there in 1497, returned to Castilla). Others fled to Italy, Greece, and Turkey. Some concealed their identities and later made their way to the New World.

Isabel sincerely believed that she was doing God's will. But her harsh treatment of both practicing Jews and *conversos* that led to the death of thousands of innocent people has left a dark stain on her reputation. Her history of cruelty and intolerance tarnishes the brilliance of her many other achievements.

In spite of the painful legacy of the Inquisition, Spain had become politically the most powerful, as well as the most admired and cultured nation in Western Europe under the inspired leadership of Queen Isabel and King Fernando. For more than a century after the death of Isabel, art and literature flourished in what is called the Golden Age of Spain.

(1) Maria of Aragon (d. 1445) (2) Isabel of Portugal (1428? – 1496)

Juan II of Castilla (1405 – 1454)

Alfonso (1453–1468)

Isabel Queen of Castilla (1451–1504)
= Fernando II King of Aragon (1452–1516)

Enrique IV (1425–1474)

(1) Blanca of Navarre (1420–1464)

(2) Juana (1439–1475)

Juana "la Beltraneja" (1461–1530)

Juan Prince of Asturias (1478–1497)
= Margaret of Austria (1480–1530)

Juana "Joanna the Mad" (1479–1555)
= Philip I King of Castilla (1478–1506)

Isabel (1470–1498)
(1) = Afonso of Portugal (1475–1491)
(2) = Manoel King of Portugal (1469–1521)

Maria (1482–1517)

Miguel (1498–1500)

Catalina Catherine of Aragon (1485–1536)
(1) = Arthur Prince of Wales (1486–1502)
(2) = Henry VIII King of England (1491–1547)

Mary Tudor Queen of England (1516–1558)

Leonor (1498–1558)

Isabel (1501–1525)
= Ferdinand I King of Hungary (1503–1564)

Maria (1505–1558)

Catalina (1507–1577)

Charles V Holy Roman Emperor (1500–1558)
= Isabel (1503–1539)

Maria (b. 1528)

Maria (1505–1558)

Juan III King of Portugal (1502–1557)

Enrique of Portugal (1512–1580)

Juana (1535–1573)

Philip II King of Spain (1527–1598)

Maria and Manoel had five other children not shown here.

The Castilian~Aragonese Family Tree

Isabel was descended from the royal families of Portugal, Castilla, and England. She was the seventh generation of daughters to have the name Isabel, going back to the thirteenth-century Portuguese queen who became a saint, Santa Isabel. Her marriage to Fernando II united the two kingdoms of Aragon and Castilla and León. Their joint rule laid the groundwork for a united España (Spain). The chart illustrates the growth of the monarchy from the fifteenth through the sixteenth century. The crown symbol indicates those who ruled. Double lines represent marriages; single lines indicate parentage. Dates of birth and deaths (where available) are noted.

Juan II of Castilla: Juan II became King of Castilla in 1419 when he was fourteen years old. In 1420 he married Maria of Aragon and after her death he married Isabel, Princess of Portugal. His rule lasted until his death in 1454.

Children of Juan II

Enrique IV: The only son of Juan II of Castilla and Maria of Aragon, he became King of Castilla and León in 1454 when he was twenty-nine years old.

Isabel of Castilla: Firstborn of Juan II and Isabel of Portugal, she married Fernando II, heir to the throne of Aragon, in 1469 and became Queen of Castilla and León in 1474. They ruled both kingdoms jointly until her death on November 26, 1504.

Alfonso XII: Born November 17, 1453, he was the second child of Juan II and Isabel of Portugal. At age thirteen, military forces proclaimed him King of Castilla. He died on July 5, 1468, probably of the plague.

Children of Isabel and Fernando II

Isabel: Firstborn of Isabel and Fernando, in 1490 she married Afonso of Portugal, who died soon after in a hunting accident. She married his uncle Manoel of Portugal in 1497 and died in childbirth a year later.

Juan: Born June 20, 1478, he married Margaret of Austria in 1497 and died that same year from a severe fever.

Juana: Known as Juana la Loca "Joanna the Mad," in 1497 she married Philip I, eldest son of the Habsburg Emperor Maximilian I. Together they ruled Castilla after her mother's death in 1504. They had six children. Son Charles was King of Spain as Charles I and Holy

Roman Emperor as Charles V. Son Ferdinand I was King of Hungary and Bohemia.

Maria: Born a twin on June 28, 1482, her sister was stillborn. She married Manoel, the widower of her sister Isabel and became Queen of Portugal. Juan, the eldest of their eight children, became King of Portugal.

Catalina: Well-known as Catherine of Aragon, in 1501 at age fifteen, she married Arthur, Prince of Wales, who died only months later. In 1509, she became the first wife of Arthur's younger brother, Henry VIII, King of England. They had one daughter, Mary Tudor.

Others in the Royal Family

Isabel of Portugal: She was seventeen years old in 1447 when she married King Juan II of Castilla, who was almost forty years old. She bore him two children, Isabel and Alfonso. After the death of her husband, she grew increasingly deranged. She died on September 22, 1496, at her home in Arévalo.

Ferdinand II: Born March 10, 1452, he was the second son of King Juan of Aragon, the first child with the

King's second wife, Juana Enríquez. He became his father's choice as heir over his older half brother, Carlos of Viana. He married his cousin, Isabel of Castilla, on October 19, 1469. He died twelve years after Isabel in 1516.

Juana of Portugal: The sister of King Afonso V, she was a sixteen-year-old princess when she married Enrique IV in May 1455. Seven years later, she gave birth to a daughter, also named Juana. Eventually, she became estranged from her husband Enrique, and she went to live in the Convent of San Francisco in Segovia, where she died in 1475.

Juana "la Beltraneja:" Born February 18, 1462, many believed she was actually the daughter of Beltrán de la Cueva, King Enrique's chief steward. She spent years in the Portuguese court trying to win her claim as true heir to the Kindgom of Castilla and León over her aunt Isabel. Isabel had her committed to the Convent of Santa Clara de Coimbra, where she died in 1530.

Engraving of a young Isabel.

Portrait of an aged Isabel. A reproduction from a painting c. 1500 by Juan de Flandes with a representation of the famed ruby and pearl jewel given to Isabel by Fernando.

Painting of King Fernando II by Bequer, from the Gallery of San Telmo, Seville.

Etching of King Enrique IV from the Bibliothèque Nationale, Paris, France. At Enrique's feet is the royal shield of Castilla (castle) and León (lion).

Engraving of Isabel's brother Alfonso XII taken from the effigy on his tomb.

Map of the Spanish states, 1266-1492. The darker shaded area is Aragon; the Kingdom of Castilla (Castile) and León, the lighter shaded area.

A modern photograph of an exterior view of the castle at Segovia. Built in the eleventh century, the castle sits high above the Eresma and Clamores rivers that meet in the valley below.

This medieval canvas portrays Jews expelled from Castilla during the Inquisition, leaving with their belongings in sacks.

This engraving from the picture by Edwin Long depicts a compulsory baptism of Moors after the conquest of Granada.

An 1893 lithograph of Christopher Columbus bidding farewell to Queen Isabel upon his departure for the New World, Friday, August 3, 1492.

A modern photograph by J. Laurent of the tombs of Catholic rulers in the royal chapel, Granada Cathedral. King Fernando II and Queen Isabel are in the foreground.

About the Author

Carolyn Meyer hated history when she was a young student. "It always seemed to be about dates and battles and generals and treaties, and I cared more about what people ate and what they wore and what they did all day." Later, when she began writing, her curiosity led her to investigate the things she most enjoyed: people in other times and other places and how they lived their lives.

Several years ago, Ms. Meyer and her husband, a historian ("He *likes* those battles and generals and treaties"), traveled to Spain and visited towns where Isabel once lived. "Segovia is a beautiful city. I can picture Isabel in that magnificent castle, and I can imagine her trying to sketch the ancient aqueduct."

As the author of more than forty books for middle-grade and young adult readers, she writes about the kind of history she loves. *Where the Broken Heart Still Beats*, *White Lilacs*, and *Gideon's People* were all named ALA Best Books for Young Adults.

Originally from Pennsylvania, Ms. Meyer now lives in New Mexico, where many descendants of Isabel's Spain live today — including some who trace their ancestry back to the Jews driven out during the terrible days of the Inquisition.

About the Spanish Language

The Spanish spoken today in Madrid has changed little since the days of Isabel and Fernando. Like French and Italian, Spanish is a Romance language, meaning that it is based on Latin, the language spoken by the Romans. It is most closely related to Portuguese; for example, *Alfonso* in Spanish is *Afonso* in Portuguese.

Unlike English, Spanish has regular rules of pronunciation: For instance, *a* is always pronounced like the *a* in *father*. The stress is on the next-to-last syllable, if the word ends in a vowel or *n* or *s*, and on the last syllable when the word ends in any consonant except *n* or *s*. When there are exceptions, an accent mark (*ó*) shows where to put the stress. A *tilde* over the *n* (*ñ*) is sounded like *ny* in *onion*.

"Castilian Spanish" differs in some ways from the Spanish spoken in the Americas: *ll* is pronounced like *lli* in *million*; *z* is sounded like *th* in *thin*; *c* before *e* and *i* are also sounded like *th*.

Here is a pronunciation guide for some of the names in this book:

Andalucía — ahn dah loo THEE ah

Aragón — ah rah GOHN

Arévalo — ah REH vah loh

Ávila — AH vee lah

Beatríz de Bobadilla — be yah TREETH deh boh bah
    DEEL yah

Beltrán de la Cueva — bel TRAHN deh lah KWEH vah

caballero — kah bahl YEHR oh

Carrillo — kah REEL yoh

Castilla — kah STEEL yah

Chacón — chah KOHN

Don, Doña — DOHN, DOH nyah

Enrique — ehn REE keh

Escorpión — eh scor pee OHN

Girón — hee ROHN

grande — GRAHN deh

Isabel — ee sah BEHL

Jimena — hee MEH nah

Juan, Juana — HWAHN, HWAHN ah

León — leh YOHN

Pacheco — pah CHEH koh

Padre — PAH dreh

Plaza Mayor — PLAH thah mah YOHR

Rodrigo Díaz de Vivar (El Cid) — rohd REE goh DEE ahth

    deh vee VAHR (el THEED)

Segovia — seh GOH vee ah

Torquemada — tohr keh MAH dah

Trujillo — troo HEEL yoh

Zaragoza — thah rah GOH thah

Zorro — THOH roh

Glossary of Characters
(* indicates fictional characters)

ISABEL'S FAMILY:

Enrique IV — Isabel's half-brother; "El León"

Alfonso — Isabel's younger brother

Queen Juana — Enrique's wife

Juana "La Beltraneja"— daughter of Enrique and Queen Juana

ISABEL'S FRIENDS AND ADVISORS:

Beatríz de Bobadilla — Isabel's friend and confidante

Andrés de Cabrera — Beatríz's fiancé, later husband

*Rodrigo — Beatríz's son

*Ana — Isabel's maid

*Ladies-in-waiting — Blanca, María, Jimena, Mencia, Elvira, Alicia

*Catalina Valera — Isabel's friend; lady-in-waiting

Archbishop Carrillo — Isabel's counselor; "El Toro"

Tomás de Torquemada — Isabel's priest and confessor

Clara — Isabel's nurse-governess

Gonzalo Chacón — Clara's husband

Gutierre de Cárdenas — Gonzalo and Clara's nephew

*Leonora — wife of Cárdenas

*Padre Guzmán — Isabel's confessor after Torquemada

Pierres de Peralta — ambassador from Aragón

María de Acuña — Carrillo's niece

Juan de Vivero — husband of María de Acuña

Isabel's suitors:

King Afonso V of Portugal — Queen Juana's brother; "El
  Escorpión"
Pedro Girón — friend of Enrique, brother of Pacheco
Prince Fernando of Aragón
Richard, Duke of Gloucester
Charles, Duke of Berry

Enrique's supporters:

Beltrán de la Cueva — Enrique's friend and advisor
Juan Pacheco — Carrillo's scheming nephew; "El Zorro"
Bishop Fonseca — supporter of Enrique and Queen Juana

Additional characters:

King Juan of Aragón — father of Fernando
*Dr. Abravanel — Isabel's physician
*Pedro Pimentel — Alfonso's friend killed in a joust

Acknowledgments

Cover painting by Tim O'Brien

Page 186: Isabel, Library of Congress.

Page 187: Isabel the Catholic, North Wind Picture Archives, Alfred, Maine.

Page 188: King Fernando II, North Wind Picture Archives, Alfred, Maine.

Page 189: King Enrique IV, Guiradon/Art Resource, New York, New York.

Page 190: Alfonso XII, Culver Pictures, Inc., New York, New York.

Page 191 (top): Map of the Spanish States, North Wind Picture Archives, Alfred, Maine.

Page 191 (bottom): The Alcazar (castle) at Segovia, Spain, SuperStock, Jacksonville, Florida.

Page 192 (top): Jews expelled from Castilla, The Granger Collection, New York, New York.

Page 192 (bottom): Compulsory baptism of Moors, North Wind Picture Archives, Alfred, Maine.

Page 193 (top): Christopher Columbus set sail, Library of Congress.

Page 193 (bottom): Tomb of Los Catolicos, Library of Congress.

Copyright © 2000 by Carolyn Meyer.
◦◦✦◦◦ ◦◦✦◦◦ ◦◦✦◦◦

All rights reserved. Published by Scholastic Inc.
555 Broadway, New York, NY 10012.
SCHOLASTIC, THE ROYAL DIARIES, and associated logos are trademarks and/or registered trademarks of Scholastic Inc.

Meyer, Carolyn.
Isabel / by Carolyn Meyer.
p. cm. — (The royal diaries)
Summary: While waiting anxiously for others to choose a husband for her, Isabel, the future Queen of Spain, keeps a diary account of her life as a member of the royal family
ISBN 0-439-07805-9
1. Isabella I, Queen of Spain, 1451–1504 — Juvenile fiction. —
2. Spain — History — Ferdinand and Isabella, 1479–1515 —
Juvenile fiction. [1. Isabella I, Queen of Spain, 1451–1504 —
Fiction. 2. Spain — History — Ferdinand and Isabella, 1479–1515 — Fiction.
3. Kings, queens, rulers, etc. — Fiction. 4. Diaries — Fiction.] I. Title.
II. Series.
PZ7.M5685Is 2000
[Fic] — dc21
99-16805
CIP

12 11 10 9 8 7 6 5 4 3 2 1   0/0 01 02 03 04

The display type was set in Callifonts Script.
The text type was set in Augereau.
Book design by Elizabeth B. Parisi
Printed in the U.S.A.   23
First printing, July 2000
◦◦✦◦◦ ◦◦✦◦◦ ◦◦✦◦◦